Losing
ROMEO

D0951456

Losing ROMEO

A.J. Byrd

Recycling programs
for this product may
not exist in your area.

LOSING ROMEO

ISBN-13: 978-0-373-83138-8

To my BFFs

Kathy Alba and Elliott Goins.
Thanks for always having my back and keeping me grounded.

Acknowledgments

To my family and friends, thanks for all the support and love that you've given me. Again to my editor, Evette Porter, thanks for lovin' my stories and being so patient with me on this project. To my wonderful fans and readers, thank you for allowing me to do what I do. It's always a pleasure to entertain you. The fan letters have been wonderful and have encouraged me to continue writing this series.

I wish you all the best of love.

BFF Rule #7

Always do what you say you're going to do.

prologue

Romeo—Teenage Dad

"What did you just say?" I ask, convinced that I heard my ex-girlfriend wrong. When she pulled me into a back room in the middle of my boy Shadiq's party, I had no way of anticipating this bomb being dropped on me. In fact, my new girlfriend, Anjenai, is outside waiting for me to return.

Phoenix sweeps her blond hair back from her face and takes a deep breath. "I said *I'm pregnant*."

"By who?"

She rolls her eyes up at me and crosses her arms. "Don't even play me. You know that you're the only one I've ever been with."

"I don't know no such thing. You're always rubbing up and flirting with some damn body."

"That was always just to make you jealous—keep you interested. You are the only one I've ever slept with."

I step away from the door and her. "Naw. Naw," I say. "This is just another one of your games. You're lying."

"I'm not lying, Romeo. I've had morning sickness since school started. It was so bad yesterday that I stayed home. I'm pregnant." She opens the small string purse on her shoulder and hands me some kind of stick.

"What the hell is that?"

"It's a pregnancy test. Read it."

I don't take the stick, but I glance down and see the word *pregnant* on a digital screen. "What? That's supposed to be proof? That just means you got a pregnant girl to piss on that thing. I didn't see you take the test."

She goes back into her purse and removes a slim object wrapped in foil. "Would you like for me to pee on it right now?"

I swallow, but nod my head. This bedroom has an adjoining bathroom. I follow her to it and watch her do the test. Less than three minutes later I'm looking at a duplicate stick with the word *pregnant* printed on it.

"Oh, shit."

Phoenix flushes the toilet and washes her hands. "Satisfied?"

"Oh, shit," I say again.

"We're going to have a baby," she states the obvious.

"Oh, shit."

"Now do you understand why I came here tonight? We have to get back together. I'm not raising this baby alone."

"Oh, shit."

"Will you *please* stop saying that?"

"I can't! Oh, shit!" I pace the floor and then stop. "We can't have a baby."

"Why the hell not?"

"We're *fifteen,*" I shout.

"That didn't stop us from having sex, now, did it?"

"Why weren't you on the pill?"

"Why didn't you use a condom?" she yells back.

My mind draws a blank as I plop down on the corner of the bed. My entire short life flashes before my eyes. "My father is going to kill me when he finds out. And that's *if* I'm lucky. My father's dreams for me are high, and he doesn't take to disappointment well."

"Don't look like that," Phoenix says. "It's not like we'll be broke and living off welfare. Our parents will help us."

I glance up at her and try to imagine being tied to her for God knows how many years while raising a baby. "I don't know what to do."

Phoenix walks over to the bed and sits down next to me. "The first thing you need to do is break it off with your new girlfriend. *Now.*"

My mind reels back to Anjenai. Sweet, smart and—importantly—drama-free Anjenai. The past few weeks I've been really getting to know her while also helping her make the girls' basketball team. And quite frankly I've been really feeling her, thinking that we'd make a great team. Now this.

"What?" Phoenix's hazel eyes tend to turn more green when she's angry and right now they look like glowing kryptonite. "I know you're not thinking about running out on your responsibilities."

I don't say anything—I can't.

Phoenix's voice starts rising. "Romeo, I didn't get pregnant by myself!"

"I know that!" I explode off the bed and start pacing again.

"Then what's the problem?" she asks, folding her arms and staring me down.

"The problem is that this is a whole lot to just be dumping on me right now." I start rubbing my hand along my jaw while I try to decide whether to yell or throw something. What the hell am I going to do with a kid at fifteen? Bump that—what the hell are my parents going to do when they find out? I have no problem picturing my father straight losing his mind. Phoenix may think our parents will help, but I think they'll kill us.

"You're not the only one who's scared here," she tells me. "I'm going to get fat!"

She says this shit with a straight face, and I'm left just staring at her. Phoenix and I have dated off and on since sixth grade. In a lot of ways it was sort of expected. We were the It couple of our class. The pretty cheerleader and the school jock—we played right into the stereotype. But things haven't been right between us for a while—a long while, if we were honest with one another. The main reason is because Phoenix likes to play too many head games. We broke up just before school started. She didn't take the break-up seriously and clearly thought that I'd boomerang back like I've done countless times before.

"I need a drink," I finally tell her and then rush out of the back room and try to shove my way through a thicket of laughing and dancing kids from school.

"Romeo, wait!" Phoenix shouts from behind me, but I don't slow up until I reach one of the high chairs in front of the breakfast bar where all the bottles of hard liquor are lined up. I pick up the bottle of Grey Goose, unscrew the top and take that sucker to the head like it is a bottle of water.

"Damn, man," some miscellaneous dude says beside me. "Is it like that?"

"You just don't know." I turn up the bottle again. I can't get drunk fast enough.

Phoenix reaches over my shoulder, grabs a shot glass and shoves it toward me. "Don't be an ass."

"Fine." I pour myself a shot instead. "Happy?"

"Romeo?"

I close my eyes and pretend that her sweet voice isn't like a switchblade stabbing me in between my ribs. "Yeah?" I don't bother to even turn around.

"What the hell are you doing?"

Phoenix turns around. "What does it look like? He's enjoying the party with his real girlfriend."

That catches everyone's attention.

"Romeo, what the hell is she talking about?" There's pain in her voice, and yet I still can't turn around. I just sit ramrod straight while my Adam's apple bobs up and down.

"Look," Phoenix says. "It's over. Romeo loves me. You had your fun. Now run along back to the hood and play with your pet rats or whatever the hell it is you poor people do."

I slam my eyes closed and imagine wrapping my hands around Phoenix's neck.

"Romeo." Anjenai flips the script, and the tough girl from Oak Hill starts seeping into her voice. "What is this bitch talking about?" I can hear her shifting from one foot to the other behind me. "What? You're going to let this bitch speak *for* you? You ain't going to man up and tell me the deal?"

It's stone cold silent in here now. Everybody is waiting to see what I'm going to do. *A baby. I'm about to be a father.* Slowly, I turn my head and lift my gaze to her angry face. The face I was just beginning to fall in love with. "I'm sorry."

"You're sorry? Damn right you're sorry. A sorry piece of shit, if you ask me," says Anjenai.

She shoves my arm hard and I nearly topple off the stool.

Phoenix jumps her skinny ass in front of me. "Leave him alone, bitch. And clean the wax out of your ears. It's *OVER!*"

"Bitch, I oughta…" Anjenai says, before she lunges straight at Phoenix and grabs two handfuls of her blond extensions.

Phoenix screams.

I jump out of my seat. "Anjenai, stop. Let her go. She's pregnant!"

There's a collective gasp inside the cottage. I pull Anjenai off Phoenix, but I must've done it with more strength than I thought because the next thing I know she's falling backwards and hitting her head on the edge of a table.

"Oh, hell, naw!" To my surprise, Tyler jumps into the

mix, swinging at my head. I go down, and Phoenix jumps on top of her.

Then Anjenai's other best friend, Kierra, springs from nowhere.

Then Phoenix's girlfriends jump into the mix and then, at last, Anjenai. No doubt about it, come Monday morning we're going to be the talk of the entire school. I'm ashamed to say that I'm getting my clock cleaned by Anjenai's fiercest friend, Tyler Jamison. In the short time since school has started, the young freshman has developed quite the reputation of being willing to fight anyone at any time, boys included. I'm trying my best not to hit a girl, but damn, she's making it hard.

It takes my boys Chris and Shadiq to step in and help a brother out. By the time I stand up from the bottom of the pile, other brothers from the football team have stepped in and are helping Shadiq drag Anjenai and her BFFs off his property.

"Anjenai." I start forward, only to have Phoenix place a restraining hand on my arm.

"Let her go," she whispers.

I shrug her hand off of me and hiss, "I, at least, owe her an explanation."

Phoenix's eyes narrow as she folds her arms. "Yeah. I'm sure you knocking me up is going to make her feel a whole lot better."

I don't think I can hate this girl any more than I do right now. "Excuse me," I say and storm away. I ignore all snickering and finger pointing as I jog to catch up with Anjenai. . "Wait! Hold up!"

"Yo, man. Let 'em go!" Chris says, marching back toward the party while the girls continue their steady march off the property. Without looking back, Anjenai jets her middle finger high in the air. Her BFFs follow suit. "Sounds like we got a lot to talk about—daddy!"

I groan and watch the best thing that has ever happened to me march away from me.

one

Phoenix—By Any Means Necessary

I have my man back. At least in theory. It's been two weeks since I dropped the news that he's about to become a father, and most times he looks at me as if he wishes that I'd never been born. I'm still sure that once he gets adjusted to the idea of becoming a father, things will go back to how they used to be. At least I hope so.

I just wish that Romeo hadn't blabbed it out to everyone when that hood rat, Anjenai, came at me. I could've handled her ass. Pregnant or not. Now all the kids at the school are tossing their two cents into our business, and I'm starting to feel more and more like I just announced I have an STD or something. Pregnancy is not contagious, I want to shout at their ignorant asses. But is Romeo catching hell about knocking me up? Hell no.

In fact, his boys elevated his ass to playa status and keep referring to me as his future baby mama. *Baby mama?* I ain't having that shit. Romeo is going to put a ring on this.

Believe that. So he might as well wipe off that long face of his and just get with the program.

At exactly five-thirty my alarm clock starts to blare my ear off, and I quickly reach over and smack the snooze button for a few more minutes. I don't know why. It's not like I got any sleep last night—or any night for the past few weeks, for that matter. Between morning sickness, stress and nerves, the last thing I've been able to do is turn my brain off and catch some Zs.

The number one thing that keeps circling in my mind? *Anjenai.* Lord knows I can't stand the bitch. Her or that pathetic crew she rolls with, which includes my traitorous half sister, Nicole. But clearly, in the short amount of time Anjenai and Romeo have been creeping together, she's managed to get inside of Romeo's head and undo years of my hard work. What happened to the Romeo who used to hang on to my every word? The Romeo who used to blow my phone up five or six times a day or offer to pick me up and drive me home from school? I swear, sometimes I don't even recognize the boy I'm dealing with now.

It's going to get better.

The minute that affirmation whispers from that small voice in the back of my head, my heart fills with doubt. Mainly because I'm too afraid to call what I see flowing between Anjenai and Romeo by its name: love. Tears burn the backs of my eyes, but I close them and the tears go away before they roll down and burn a hole in my pillow.

The alarm goes off for a second time and of course I hit the snooze button again. Maybe I shouldn't even bother going to school today. I'm not really in the mood to put up with all the BS people are shoveling my way. That includes from my own two best friends, Raven and Bianca. The three of us are known as the Redbones at school. Contrary to popular opinion, it wasn't a name that we selected, but one that was thrust on us by a bunch of haters who, deep down, wanted to be like us: beautiful.

But here's something that most of those wannabes don't know about my clique. The last people we trust is each other. For all the years that we've been friends, I know for a fact those heifers aren't any better than those project hoes spilling out of Oak Hill. At the first opportunity, either one of them will stab me in the back if it means that she can be on top—which is why I don't tell them everything.

They learned about the pregnancy the same time everyone at the party did. That didn't go over so well, and now they have about as much of an attitude as Romeo. Whatever. They can all just kiss my ass.

Now they think I don't notice that every time I walk up on them they stop whispering and just flash me those robotic smiles. I'm not dumb. I taught them that slick-ass move. Whatever. If need be they can take a time-out and stay the hell up out of my face like the rest of the school's haters. All that matters is that I got my man back.

Another wave of tears threatens to spill just as my alarm clock goes off for the third time. I finally turn the alarm off and find the strength to climb out of bed. The moment I do, this unbelievable sharp pain first hits me in my lower back but then quickly wraps around my entire abdomen. "Aah."

I reach over and grab hold of my chest of drawers because

my knees are, like, two seconds from buckling and dropping me to the floor. "What the…?"

There's a knock on my door before I hear my mother's chipper voice, "Phoenix, honey. It's time to get up."

I can barely breathe, but somehow I manage to croak out, "I'm up," in order to make her get away from my door. Panting profusely I wait for her to walk away. When she does, it's just a small measure of relief because this pain is now making me see a mobile of stars circling around my head. I struggle to get to the bathroom, but it's sort of like an inchworm traveling from Georgia to Texas.

A couple of lifetimes later, I make it, huffing and puffing. Seconds later, I feel something wet leaking down between my legs. I look down and I'm horrified at the sight of brownish red blood spotting the pink-tiled floor.

"Oh, my God. No." Another stab of pain hits, and my mouth drops open but I can't even manage to get any sound past my lips this time. I'm miscarrying or dying—one or both. Honestly, I'm hoping it's the latter because losing this baby will throw a big monkey wrench into my plans.

I get to the toilet and peel off my soaked panties only to hear clots of blood hit the water with sickening splashes. I can no longer hold back my tears, now that it's clear to me exactly what's happening.

No baby.

No Romeo.

The very idea of losing him again causes my abdomen to lock up even tighter. He'll leave me. I know he will. Hell, it's clear that he wants to leave now, when he thinks I'm having his baby. It's just his word that he's going to man up and be here for me and our child. That's all that's binding him to me. And if there's one thing I know well about the love of my life, it's that he always does what he says he's going to do.

An hour later, I'm sitting in a tub of hot water and I'm just trying to think. But all I'm successful in doing is crying. No way I'm going to school just so that I can act like everything is fine—especially since everything is far from being fine. At a time like this, I wish more than anything that there was someone I could really talk to. Someone I could trust to keep their damn mouth shut. Unfortunately, I don't know anyone like that.

Fleetingly, I think about how it would be nice to talk to my mother about this. But let's face it. My mother is many things, but deep ain't one of them. Shopping, brunches and gossiping is the extent of her expertise. My mom's main job is to be beautiful. Why? Because my father loves beautiful things.

Growing up, my father would always joke about how lucky I am because he's rich and my mother is good-looking. I grew up believing that I was an honest-to-God princess. Daddy dearest bought me everything he thought I wanted and made sure that everyone respected the pedestal he perched me on. Of course, the one thing I truly wanted, to spend more time with him, he made it clear a long time ago that I simply couldn't have.

Why? Work. The excuse of the century. Let him tell it, he works 24/7. I don't buy it, and I don't think my mother does, either. But at least he hasn't brought home any more brothers and sisters. My brain finally stops at Nicole, my pain-in-the-ass half sister. We may share the same dad, but we're nothing alike. For one thing, the girl has to be twice my size, fashion challenged and always showing up at the most embarrassing time. Bottom line: I hate her.

I shouldn't be surprised that she sided with Anjenai last night, but in a strange way I am and I'm a little hurt, too. I draw in a deep breath and notice for the first time that the water is starting to cool. I'm cramping, but at least the bleeding has stopped. I still have to clean up the mess before the maid sees it and reports it to my mother. But not right now. I still need a plan.

It's hours later, after I've cleaned up and spent most of the time ignoring phone calls and text messages, that the answer starts staring me in the face. I run the idea through my head again, checking for loopholes or ways this miracle plan could backfire or blow up in my face. Honestly, there's a few possible ways that either or both could happen, but hell, I'm a desperate girl, here.

An image of Romeo and Anjenai together again floats across my mind. *This plan has to work.* "It will work," I reaffirm aloud. Keeping Romeo is worth any risk coming my way.

two

Anjenai—Un-Break My Heart

I hate Romeo. I hate that I ever met him. I hate that I ever trusted him. And I hate that I was stupid enough to allow my seeing him to come between me and my two best friends in the whole world, Kierra and Tyler. For God's sake, we've been together for, like, forever. We went to day care together. Through thick and thin, we've always had each other's backs. The three chains around our necks, *B-F-F*, are supposed to remind us of that fact every day.

I lost track of that.

But it'll never happen again.

Romeo Blackwell is dead to me. So he may as well stop trying to stare a hole into the side of my head in Spanish class and in gym. Besides, I don't know why he's looking like he wants to talk to me so bad. He's the one who dumped me in the middle of my first high school party. He's the one who had my friends and me looking like a bunch of loud project hood rats who dared to show up in their rich kids' suburban paradise.

The truth of the matter is that my side of town was re-zoned and we were forced to go to Maynard Jackson High complete with all these stuck-up divas and wannabe ballers. They are all so tired that it's not even funny.

"Ms. Legend?" Ms. Lopez inquires.

I quickly jar back to my second-period class and realize that all eyes in the classroom are focused on me. "Yes?"

Ms. Lopez looks annoyed. "I called on you to recite the days of the week in Spanish."

Now I'm annoyed and quickly rattle off, *"Lunes, martes, miércoles, jueves, viernes, sábado y domingo."*

"Very good," she says and moves on to someone else who's not paying attention in her class.

I'm being pissy and I know it. I'm not normally like this. I'm usually the annoying smart chick who studies all the time, makes the honor roll and obsesses about grades and scholarships even though I'm just a freshman. Mainly because, unlike most of the kids in this school, I don't have parents who will be able to write big tuition checks to the college of my choice when I get out of here.

Hell, I don't have parents at all. They were killed in a car accident. Now my four brothers and I live with Granny on a fixed income. It's not easy, given how small Granny's apartment is. We're all packed in there like a can of sardines. We don't have much, but we have each other. I may go to Maynard Jackson High, but I don't belong here.

The class bell rings and Tyler and I jump out of our chairs like Pop Tarts in a toaster.

"Whoa," Tyler says, grabbing my arm. "Slow your roll.

Don't let that asshole chase you out of here." She gives Romeo an evil look with a sideward glance.

She's right. I slow down and smile at her.

"What?" Tyler asks.

I shrug and say simply, "I'm just glad that we're cool again."

Tyler gets this goofy smile on her face and then playfully bumps my shoulder. Our first month here at this school had managed to do something that we never thought could happen: pull us apart. On our first day of school, Tyler, Kierra and I had all developed a crush on Romeo. Instead of letting a boy come between us, we'd all agreed that none of us would go after him. It seemed like an easy deal to make, considering the chances of the most popular boy in the school actually falling for one of us were slim to remote.

That is, until Coach Whittaker encouraged Romeo to help me work out for basketball tryouts. I could shoot, but running and dribbling were horses of different colors. Still, everything was cool until that first practice, when Romeo kissed me. Remembering that kiss now fills me with so many mixed emotions that I can hardly think straight.

"Are you all right?" Tyler asks probably because my smile turned into a frown in the blink of an eye.

"Yeah. Yeah. I'm cool," I lie. "I'll see you at lunch."

Tyler bobs her head, but she studies me for another second before taking off to her English class.

I, on the other hand, just suck in a deep breath and head to my locker. The very moment I finish messing with the combination to my lock, Romeo steps up to me. "We need to talk."

His voice is like warm honey dripping in my ear. For a split second, I want to forgive him. I want to pretend that he and Phoenix didn't embarrass and humiliate me and my friends at Shadiq's party. I want to forget that he's fifteen and is about to become Phoenix's baby daddy by the summer.

"I know that you're mad," he continues.

I don't even glance his way. One look at his honey-brown skin, deep dimples and warm brown eyes and I might just melt. Hell, I think I'm doing that anyway.

Romeo continues. "I'm sorry. You have no idea how sorry I am about—"

"Oh, I have a pretty good idea of *exactly* how sorry you are," I hiss, grabbing my history book and slamming my locker door. "The good news is I just don't give a damn." I jerk away from him, and I'm surprised when he grabs my arm. Even then I refuse to look at him. "Take your hands off me."

"Anjenai," he whispers. "It's killing me to think that you hate me."

I jerk my arm from his grasp. "Get used to it." I storm away with my head held high, but my stomach is looping in knots. I hope he doesn't think I'm stupid and don't know that the reason that he chose today to speak to me is that Phoenix isn't here today. He's just a lapdog without a leash.

I'm over it.

three

Tyler—Bad Girl

I don't like English class, so at the last second I decide to ditch it and play hooky. There's no point in hanging out by the bleachers. Coaches and teachers are cracking down on kids skipping class over there. Loitering in the girls' bathrooms is no fun because Nance, the security guard, patrols this place like it's a prison which I guess it is. No. I think I'll just take a hike down the road a bit and hang out at the strip mall a few blocks down the way. Besides, the walk would probably go a long way toward clearing my mind. Don't get me wrong, I'm relieved that Anje and I have been able to squash that silly-ass beef between us. Looking back on it, knowing what I know, I can't believe that we were ever fighting over that loser or that I even made that whack-ass attempt to steal him.

Hindsight is always *twenty-twenty.*

As boldly as you please, I trek across school property, not giving a damn if the powers that be see me or not, and then head on down the road toward the strip mall. All the while, I keep replaying that one kiss I laid on Romeo. It was even more humiliating when I realized that he wasn't kissing me back. I really put myself on the line only to have him tell me how sorry he was but that he was really into Anje instead of me. Just goes to prove that you can't believe anything anyone says anymore. It also didn't help that Phoenix's high-yella hoes, Bianca and Raven, rolled up on us and blabbed to the whole school what they saw. It got around to Anjenai, and for a few weeks, we went from being friends to enemies. It was the first time in our fourteen-year history.

I have to be honest with myself—that was one of the lowest times in my life. And that's saying something. With my mom walking out on my dad and me and my dad working so much that half the time I think he forgets that I even exist, the last thing I needed was to lose the friendship that had always been the one constant in my life. And the whole damn thing would have been my fault.

Honestly, sometimes I think I can't help the dumb stuff I do. My biggest problem is my temper. But knowing that and being able to control it seem to be two *very* different things. I can't help it that everything annoys me—people in particular, and my damn school coming in a close second. I should just drop out. Sure, I'm happy that I made the basketball team. But how long will that last, since I have to maintain a C average and my ass don't even like going to class? I swear to God, this place is just trying to bore me to death. It takes everything I have to not put toothpicks in my eyelids to prop them open just to stay awake.

Maybe things would have been different if Oak Hill kids

hadn't been rezoned to come out to this suburban nightmare and instead we went to Riverwood High like Anje, Kierra and I had been planning since we were in grade school. I can't stand being around these black bourgie sellouts.

I should drop out.

I want to drop out.

Hell. It's not like my father would ever know. He doesn't know half of what I do. If he did, it would probably give him a heart attack. I can't help chuckling at that. Then I draw in a deep breath and exhale slowly. There's a part of me that knows that I shouldn't be so hard on my dad. After all, he did come to my rescue that night at Shadiq's party and pick me up from that lone dark road. That was cool. But after that, he went right back to being an MIA dad and I went back to feeling like a ghost in our apartment. We hardly speak, talk or even remain in the same room together when he's home.

Yeah, I know that jobs are tight and he has to hold on to whatever piece of job that he has at all costs, but most of the time I just feel like…the world has forgotten about me. My damn mother definitely did. She just packed up and left like we suddenly didn't matter anymore. I know that was hard on my dad, too. For a long time after she left, there wasn't a liquor bottle he didn't like. That's when I started to feel like he'd walked out on me, as well.

It still feels that way. To this day, he's never really sat down and tried to explain to me what happened. Sure, they fought all the time. She'd scream. He'd yell. Things were thrown, and in the end a door was slammed with the words, "I'll be back in a minute."

I didn't get it.

I still don't.

For a long time I was in denial, thinking that she just left to teach him a lesson and that she was going to come back. He was going to apologize, and we could go back to being the dysfunctional family that we'd always been. When that didn't happen, I thought that I was really the cause of her leaving and no one had the guts to tell me. Eventually, she mailed my father a letter, but he never let me read it. I want to know what it said, but now I lack the guts to ask my dad to see it.

After the sadness and then the depression, I started to feel resentment and then anger. I seem to be stuck on angry.

My dad's drinking eventually subsided. He slips up every now and then. But I do recognize that he's trying to reconnect. But honestly? I still feel like it's a little too late.

"Ayo, Tyler! Wait up!" a voice yells out to me. "Where you goin'?"

I jerk around to see Michelle and Trisha plodding their way toward me. Looks like I'm not the only one that decided to skip class. "Nowhere," I holler back and then shrug my shoulders when they catch up with me. "I was just kickin' it."

Michelle and Trisha are also Oak Hill girls, aka hood rats, according to our bourgie classmates. I guess you can say we're sort of friends, even though I broke their one-time leader, Billie Grant's, nose on the first day of school. At first I thought that made me enemy number one, but it turned out that Billie wasn't all that well liked within her own clique. That or there's just no loyalty nowadays.

Anyway, I started hanging with Michelle and Trisha during the time Anje and I were beefing. I guess they are all right. They introduced me to a few things—nothing too serious—experimenting with marijuana and stuff. But I don't trust them any farther than I can throw them.

"What are y'all doing out here?"

"We saw you sneaking off the school grounds, so we figured we'd just catch up and hang with you."

I nod even though I'm not really in the mood for company. My annoyance disappears when I see Michelle reach into her jean jacket and pull out a fat blunt and a lighter right here in the open. She's bold like that.

"Want a hit?" she asks, lighting up and taking a couple of tokes.

"Hell, why not?" I say. I'm bold like that, too. I take a few puffs and then pass it over to Trisha. I hold the smoke in my lungs for as long as I possibly can, and as I exhale, the thick smoke clouds take away all the stress I was feeling a few minutes ago.

Michelle and Trisha start talking a bunch of trash that I'm not a bit interested in, so I end up just nodding my head through most of it. All that matters is that they keep the rotation going. By the time we reach the strip mall we are all high and giggling like a group of six-year-olds.

Once we reach the mall, we start perusing one of the department stores. I start wondering why the hell I even bothered coming here. It's not like I have any money or anything. Not that I would have anywhere near what it costs for even a T-shirt. Still, I sift through the stuff with a mix of disgust and longing. I can easily picture the Redbones strutting in here and plopping down one of their parents' stupid credit cards to buy whatever the hell their hearts want.

For a few minutes I drift away from Michelle and Trisha. But when I circle back, I'm stunned to see them stuffing clothes in their bags, down their pants and under their jackets.

"What are y'all doing?" I hiss.

"Shh," Michelle says. "Just keep an eye out."

Oh, shit. My high is instantly blown. They are straight jacking the place, I realize. My nervous gaze skitters about. I see two salespeople helping out customers and one lady checking someone out at the cash register. "Hurry up," I say.

I gotta hand it to Michelle and Trisha—they clearly look like professionals: snipping off price tags and security tags with impressive precision. Five minutes later, we're strolling out the joint, smiling like three little angels. I ain't gonna lie: my heart is racing like crazy. The blunt we smoked is probably adding to my paranoia. Not until we make it outside the mall do I relax, but even then I half expect a security guard to jump out of nowhere and haul our asses to jail.

When the coast is clear, I look at them. "Damn. You two might want to warn a bitch before you pull a stunt like that."

"I thought that was a given," Trisha says, laughing. "What else are you supposed to do at a mall?"

Michelle laughs and then smacks her lips. "I already got the munchies."

Across the way is a Taco Bell. With just one glance at the place, my stomach starts growling. "Yeah. I can eat. We ain't going to steal tacos, too, are we?"

"HEY, YOU GIRLS! STOP RIGHT THERE!"

My head jerks back to the front of the mall to see a team of security guards charging toward us.

Michelle yells, "RUN!"

Hell, she doesn't have to say it twice.

four

Kierra—Regret

IT'S what I see and feel whenever I see Christopher Hunter, one of Romeo's road dawgs. I regret that I ever met him, talked to him, kissed him and I definitely regret that I ever had sex with him if you want to call what we did sex. Hell, it all happened so fast, I can't be too sure. I just know there was a lot of pain and tears. After that, the asshole was running out of the bedroom door so fast he left skid marks. Judging by the way he's acting, I'd say that he feels the same way about me. If you ask me, Romeo and Chris are definitely two birds of a feather.

I haven't told anybody about what happened, and I don't plan to, either. So far it looks like he's kept his big mouth shut, too. In a strange way, I'm both relieved and hurt at the same time. But with all this talk about Phoenix being pregnant I'm starting to worry that that pathetic performance might turn me into a baby mama, too. God, I hope not.

More than anything, I'm mad at myself. Now, I'm not going to sit here and claim to be so self-righteous that I was waiting for my wedding night to lose my virginity, but I was hoping that my first time would be with someone special. I'm not saying that I believe Christopher was that guy…I mean, I think I was more or less overwhelmed that someone from the cool set was paying me any attention. After all, Anjenai had Romeo, so why couldn't I attract his best boy? In truth, the whole evening went so fast. We were kissing, his tongue was down my throat and the next thing I knew he was taking me to a bedroom where the lights were out. I don't know how I lost control of the situation. In the end, I can't claim that Chris forced himself on me or anything like that. The bottom line is that everything happened too fast. Afterwards he treated me like trash.

I sniff, and Nicole, who I forgot was walking beside me, glances over at me. "Are you all right?"

"Yeah. I'm fine," I lie and glance over. "So where's your sister today?"

Nicole rolls her eyes. "Half sister," she reminds me. "I don't know. I don't keep tabs on what the hell she does."

There's no question that Nicole and Phoenix have no love lost between them. In a lot of ways it's kind of hard to believe that they're even related. Whereas Phoenix is this ultra-evil skinny bitch, Nicole is an overly sweet, plus-size klutz just struggling to fit in somewhere—anywhere. Sure, she can be a little annoying from time to time with her overeagerness, but you can't help but like her. She gets mad respect for jumping into that fight at the party. It takes a lot to go against your own sister. Since that time the BFFs have adopted her. She's officially a part of our group. We've never done that before. Sure, we have other friends outside of our group, but we've never invited any of them into our close circle. Loyalty means a lot to us.

"Why are you asking about Phoenix?"

"I don't know. I guess I was just wondering if having the whole school gossip about her situation was getting to her."

"Oh, please. Phoenix loves being the center of attention. I wouldn't put it past her if this was part of some huge master plan to sink her claws back into Romeo."

"What? You think she's faking a pregnancy to get him back? Wouldn't that be a little—"

"Extreme?"

"I was going to say crazy."

"It could be either or both," Nicole laughs.

"You know her better than I do, but I don't see it. The type of gossip going around isn't what I imagine her risking her spot on the varsity cheerleading squad over."

Nicole shrugged. "Good point. I hadn't thought about that."

"You hadn't?"

"Nope."

"When was the last time you saw a pregnant cheerleader bouncing around, yelling, 'Give me an *R!*'?"

Nicole laughs.

I can tell that the idea of Phoenix losing her spot on the varsity squad is tickling her fancy. Her smile is stretching wider than her face. We enter the cafeteria as I remember how disastrous it was for Nicole when she tried out with me for the freshman cheerleading squad. Let's just say grace and coordination aren't exactly my girl's strong suits. She landed on the pep squad instead.

"Has she told her parents?" I ask. "About the pregnancy, I mean."

"I doubt it. I'm not aware of my father having a heart attack—which he will when he finds out."

"And you haven't been tempted to drop a dime on her yourself?" I'm not advocating that she try to induce a heart attack in her father, but given how much Phoenix has made her life a living hell, I'd figure that Nicole would leap at the chance to kick Phoenix off that high-ass pedestal their father has her perched on.

"Believe me. I thought about it. And if it wasn't for people's tendency to shoot the messenger I would have called him that night after we were kicked out the party. Nah. This is Phoenix's mess, and I want no part of it. Besides," she adds after thinking about it for a second, "I think my father would force them to get married, and *that* would be just up Phoenix's alley."

"Really?"

"Either that or tell her to get an abortion. I can't decide which."

My heart drops. "What? You really think that he would do that?"

"If she's not too far along. Maybe. He wouldn't like the idea of having a pregnant teenage daughter. It would reflect badly on him."

"Even if it was you?"

"What—the bastard child? That's a horse of a different color."

It's right on the tip of my tongue to ask whether that means she believes that her father campaigned for her mother to terminate her pregnancy with her, but I manage to catch myself and not go there. Still, the idea of being forced to have an abortion is appalling to me and has me hating her father over a hypothetical situation. Go figure.

"That still leaves open the possibility that Phoenix got pregnant on purpose," Nicole says.

Now, that blows my mind. "You think she would really do something like that?"

"I wouldn't put *anything* past Phoenix. I mean. C'mon. Every idiot knows that it just takes one time to get pregnant. Right? Why didn't they have any protection?"

My heart sinks. "Right."

BFF Rule #8

Stay true in good times and in bad.

five

Nicole—*Watching from the Sidelines*

I ain't even going to lie. The idea that Phoenix's perfect world may be crashing down around her head is doing nothing but putting a smile on my face. After all, the blood flowing between us has never meant much to her, so why should it mean anything to me? God knows that I've tried I don't know how many times to be a true sister—let alone a friend—only to have my efforts laughed at and ridiculed.

To be truthful, I have thought about dropping a dime on Phoenix several times, in fact. But what I told Kierra is the truth. People shoot the messenger all the time. Of course, there is that thin possibility that if my father is disappointed in Phoenix he will then start looking toward me a little more favorably, but the chances of that are so minuscule that it's not really worth the risk.

I'm not as pretty as Phoenix, and my failed attempt to land on the cheerleading squad has done more damage to my ego than I tend to let on, but none of that means that somehow I deserve less love. The situation with my father is best described as: f—ed up.

My father, a successful and upstanding member in the world of finance once upon a time, strayed from his wife's bed, had an affair with my mother and ta-da. My mom, more or less, uses me to get money, jewelry and whatever else she can think of out of him. As far as receiving love, nurturing and all that other good stuff, I can hang it up. I swear it seems like I spend half my life wishing that I was Phoenix. She is the one who lives in the big fancy house, has her own car at fifteen and is latched onto the arm of the captain of the football team. Could it get any more perfect than that?

It's all superficial, and it's all not supposed to mean anything. Blah. Blah. But isn't that just what people who don't have those things tell themselves so they can feel better? If I'm wrong, it certainly doesn't feel that way.

As for my parents, they're not supposed to still be messing around. At least, that's the lie that they try to keep selling to Phoenix and her mother. I keep my mouth shut about that, too. What can I say? I'm just a treasure trove of secrets. No one expects me to talk, but I certainly dream about it.

I bet that would get everyone's attention. Phoenix's mother would stop pretending I don't exist. Phoenix would stop the Redbones from picking on me. And my dad... that's a big blank. I don't know what to hope for with our relationship.

The person who has always been nice to me, surprisingly, is Romeo. And he never allowed his boys Chris and Shadiq to talk out the sides of their necks toward me. Which is why I think I'm genuinely surprised how that whole ugliness at Shadiq's party went down. It seems completely out of character for him to treat Anjenai like he did. I'm more than disappointed in him. Seeing that side of him, I now think that he and Phoenix deserve one another.

I don't have any regrets coming to the BFFs' defense that night. The BFFs are the only real friends I've ever had. Actually, it felt pretty good to finally fight back. I reach out and grab my slice of pizza. Before I shove it into my mouth. I catch a strange look from Kierra.

"What?" I ask her.

Kierra's little shoulders bob up and down. "Nothing." She stabs her salad and then shovels it into her mouth.

Anjenai plops down next to us. "Where's Tyler?" she asks.

"Don't know," I say. "I haven't seen her since first period."

"Humph!" Anjenai pulls out her brown-bag lunch and proceeds to attack the bologna sandwich.

"I'm sure she's around here somewhere," Kierra says, unconcerned. "Most likely she's in the principal's office for fighting with someone again."

I nod, because in the short time that I've known Tyler, I've learned that the girl loves to fight for any and all reasons.

"I don't think we can talk," Anjenai observes. "Seeing how we tend to get in just as many."

"That's because we're her backup," Kierra points out.

"Exactly."

We all share a chuckle.

"Eventually, we're going to have to talk to her about all this fighting," Kierra says.

I laugh. "What? Like an intervention?"

"Something. Tyler is just begging to go to juvie, and I ain't trying to go out like that."

"It's not *that* bad," Anjenai says.

"You're in denial," Kierra retorts. "It doesn't help that she's been spending a lot of time with Michelle and Trisha—you know, the girls who used to hang with Billie Grant."

"You're kidding," Anjenai says.

Kierra shrugs. "That's what I heard."

We stare at her like she just told us that she believes in UFOs. Anjenai's gaze shifts over to me. "Have you heard about this?"

"I think I've seen her with Michelle in the hallway before, but I didn't think that they were friends friends, you know."

"Are you sure?" Anje asks Kierra again.

"Yeah. They were hanging out pretty heavy during the time that y'all two were really beefing. I thought it was strange, but dismissed it."

Anje glances back over to me. "Maybe we do need an intervention."

"That's going to go well," I say dubiously. The first time I ever met Tyler she was talking wild and putting Romeo in his place when he stepped to her. For a minute there, I actually thought that he had a thing for Tyler and not An-jenai. In fact, I was sure of it. The way things are shaping up I'll need a flowchart to keep up with this high-school soap opera.

"Okay," Anje says, clapping her hands together. "How about we plan a sleepover at her place, since her father is always gone and there's no room at my place."

Kierra shook her head. "I have to watch McKenya at night while Deborah's working. Let's have it at my place." She turns to me. "Think you can come?"

The very idea of a sleepover thrills me. I've never been invited to a sleepover. "Sure. When?"

"How about this weekend? Saturday night?"

"Count me in," I say, probably a little too eager to spend my first night in the projects. That must be what leads me to ask, "It is safe, isn't it?"

Kierra and Anjenai laugh.

My face reddens with embarrassment, I say, "Okay. Stupid question. Forget I asked."

I glance down at my tray, and I'm surprised to see that I've eaten everything without realizing it. That's been happening a lot. I eat, but I never really get full. One thing's for sure, my clothes are definitely getting tighter. Maybe I'll go on a diet tomorrow. But I kind of tell myself that every day. I'll start tomorrow. I'll start tomorrow. That's the story of my life.

The truth is, the minute I tell myself that I'm on a diet and I can't have something sweet or fattening, then all of a sudden I want it ten times more. Diets don't last just a couple of days with me. They last just a couple of *hours*. The bottom line is that I'm an emotional eater. I eat when I'm sad. I eat when I'm stressed. I eat when I'm bored.

The bell rings, and we all pop out of our chairs like jack-in-the-boxes.

"This weekend," Anjenai says. "Don't forget."

I grab my tray and rush over to stack it with the other dirty trays next to the garbage cans. When I'm halfway there, a pair of voices drifts over to me.

"Did you see how much food she put away? That girl is like a human garbage disposal."

Laughter.

I turn and glance over my shoulder to see Bianca and Raven.

"What?" Raven challenges. "You got something to say, wide-ass?" The people at the table they're standing next to start a ripple of laughter.

They turn and walk away, and I stand there like a fool while tears streak down my face.

SIX

Romeo—Trapped

It's killing me that she won't talk to me—even though I can't blame her. I did take her to Shadiq's party and then abandon her to talk to Phoenix. The way the whole situation went down, I was more shocked about becoming a father than anything else—I'm still in shock. I wish I knew how to fix all of this. If I could just get five minutes alone with her. No interruptions and without a whole school of kids milling around us, so I can just explain what happened that night. Even then I don't think it would do any good. What I did was pretty messed up.

How many ways can someone say that they're sorry? How many times? What will it take for the other person to believe you?

"Damn, man. You got it bad."

I glance up to see Shadiq, who's smiling and shaking his head. "What?"

"You heard me. You got it bad. I mean, damn, have you even heard a word we've said in the last five minutes?"

I glance to my right to see Chris looking at me and shaking his head.

"C'mon. You know I got a lot on my mind."

"Yeah. It looks like you still have Anjenai on your mind," Shadiq concludes as we herd out of the cafeteria and head toward the gym.

"You're a strange brother," Chris says. "I'll tell you that. Exactly how many baby mamas are you trying to make, anyway?" he laughs.

"Ha. Ha. You're a regular Chris Rock."

"Me? You were the one trying to stare a damn hole in the girl's head during lunch. Shit. If you want to talk to her so bad, why didn't you just walk your ass over there? Or were you scared she and her girls were going to open another can of whup-ass on you?" He and Shadiq laughed.

I just shake my head because I don't have a defense. I did want to go over and try to talk to Anjenai again, but feared she or her girls would make a scene. Isn't that the reason girls travel in packs?

"Aw." Chris nods. "Li'l bookworm won't give you the time of day now, huh?"

"Man, get out my face with that nonsense."

"Shit. Have you seen yourself lately?"

To my right, Shadiq lifts his camera phone and snaps a picture. He takes a look, shakes his head and then shows it to me. "Crying shame, man. You need to pull it together before people start thinking you're in love with someone other than your baby mama."

They crack up again while I swat the phone away. "I got ninety-nine problems, and y'all are two of them."

My boys continue to laugh at my silly ass as we enter the boys' locker room to dress up for gym. "Why are you giving me a hard time, anyway?" I say to Chris. "Didn't you go to the party with Anje's girl Kierra?"

The smile fell off Chris's face. I must have hit a sore spot.

"Man, forget that l'il bitch. She ain't about nothing but wasting a brother's time."

"Ah. That must mean that she didn't give you none," Shadiq howls.

"Sheiiit." Chris twists up his face. "When have you ever known me to strike out? I don't play that. I'm the original panty dropper."

Me and Shadiq crack the hell up over that.

"Nah. Nah, man. I'm being for real." Chris's chest swells up as he boasts. "I hit that shit at the party."

My laugh fades a bit as I try to evaluate whether he's telling the truth or not.

"Puh-lease," Shadiq says. "We supposed to believe that you was with that girl and you ain't said shit about it? I ain't never known you to hold water."

Chris shrugs his shoulders as he opens his locker. "What's there to tell? I hit it and split it. That's a regular Friday night for me."

"Man, you're full of shit," Shadiq concludes.

Our disbelief seems to agitate Chris. "Nah, man. I'm being straight up. That girl was all over me that night. The shit didn't come no easier. I gave her a little something to drink so she could get her buzz on, we started sucking on each other's necks and then I led her to one of the bedrooms and pounded her into the headboard for a few minutes." He tossed up his hands like he'd scored a touchdown. "Now what y'all know about that?"

I look Chris up and down and I think I'm starting to believe him. "Sooo what happened? You slept with the girl and then turned around and kicked her out of the party?" I ask, trying to wrap my brain around what he was saying.

Chris shrugs his shoulders. "Hell, I was done."

"Did you use protection?" I ask.

"What the…? Did *you?*" Chris laughs in my face. "How you gonna clock me? You're the only baby daddy in this group."

"That's exactly why I'm checking you. Don't you think one is one too many?"

"Whoa. Don't be pinning your problem on me, man. Besides, the way I see it, if these chicks ain't on birth control, that ain't our fault."

Okay, now I can't believe what I'm hearing. "What?"

"C'mon, man," Chris whines and shakes his head. "These chicks know what we're about. If they don't, then that is called bad parenting. Hell, we're fifteen. We're supposed to have just one thing on our minds. And frankly, most of these girls are just as horny as we are. Kierra wanted it just as much as I did, but she gonna sit up there and start crying."

"WHAT?" Shadiq and I thunder.

"Nah, man. I'm just saying." He shrugs.

"She was *crying?*" I ask for clarification.

"How was I to know that she was a virgin? She wasn't acting like one."

Before I can even think straight I have my boy jacked up against the wall. "Did you rape her?"

"WHAT? Hell, naw, man!"

Everyone in the locker room freezes.

Chris tries to push back. "Let go of me, man. What the hell is wrong with you? How you gonna accuse me of some bullshit like that? That ain't how it went down." He glances over my shoulder at Shadiq. "What, you gonna just stand there? Help get him off me."

Shadiq shakes his head like he doesn't want any part of this.

"Why don't you concentrate on answering my questions," I bark.

Chris looks me dead in my eye and states, "NO. I DID NOT!"

No lie, I'm torn between throwing a punch and letting this slide. But after staring him down for a while, I decide that he's telling the truth and let him go. I watch as he slides back down the wall.

"Damn, man," Chris croaks. "What's up with you? You gonna tell me that you got the hots for Kierra, too?"

"Man, close your mouth and calm your ass down," I say, turning away. The moment I do I hear him trying to rush me, but Shadiq quickly steps in between us and shoves him back against the wall.

"You heard him. Calm down."

"Oh. It's like that?" Chris accuses, looking hurt.

Realizing that Chris needs to save face, Shadiq puts him in a playful headlock. "Chill. Man, you know that we're just messing with you," he says with a laugh. "You know we're boys."

Everyone relaxes, believing that beef was our way of joking around. He releases Chris, but Chris still doesn't look too pleased.

"Boys, huh?" His gaze shifts back and forth between me and Shadiq. "You can't prove that by me." He grabs his stuff and storms off.

We just watch him go.

"Think he'll calm down?" I ask.

Shadiq shrugs his shoulders. "Yeah. He'll be all right." He returns his attention to me. "I did think that you were going to bust one square in his mouth, though." He laughs. "Just how many chicks are you juggling?"

"Not funny," I say, rushing to change clothes.

"I wasn't trying to be funny."

"Kierra is a nice girl," I say.

"*And* she's Anjenai's best friend," he adds.

"So?" I snap.

"I'm just saying."

I drop the subject and finish changing. When he heads on down to the gym, Shadiq asks, "So what are you and Phoenix going to do?"

"Man, I don't have the slightest damn idea."

There's a slight pause before Shadiq says, "Look. I ain't trying to start nothing between you and your girl, but—"

I glance over at him. "What? Come on with it."

"I don't know." He shrugs, clearly uncomfortable with this subject. "Do you think that she did this shit on purpose?"

"What do you mean?"

"Well, you know how Phoenix is. Don't you find it a little convenient that she gets pregnant just when you two break it off?"

I laugh. "Entrapment?"

"Yeah. Shit. My dad tells me all the time to never put anything past a female. You know what I'm saying? This stuff happens all the time—especially to athletes. If a girl thinks that you have the potential to be something, she tries to sink her claws in you early. Now I know that sounds like some sexist shit but it's held up by the facts."

I just look at him.

"You don't think that Phoenix isn't above trying to trap you with a baby?"

I don't even want to answer that.

"Well, you just marinate in it for a little while."

We exchange dabs.

In the gym, Coach Whittaker and her assistant are talking to this new dude I ain't seen before. "Who that?"

Shadiq looks up. "Oh. New kid. Transferred down here from New York. He's in my homeroom. His dad is in the music entertainment business and starting a label down here."

"What's his name?"

"Kwan something or another."

I note the strange look in Shadiq's eye. "What? Is the dude a rapper or something?" I ask only because Shadiq's love outside of football is music. He's been plotting and planning his debut in the rap game since we were in elementary school. He views anyone who claims that he can rhythm as an enemy.

"I don't know. He says that he can flow and shit."

"Oh. So you want a battle."

"If the boy thinks that he can spit, why not?"

I give the new dude another glance and check out his style and shine. I have to admit the boy is representing. And judging by the way the girls are giggling and pointing he's going to be some serious competition for some of the fellahs. "Before you think about battling him, maybe you need to find out what his connect is."

Shadiq frowns.

"I mean, if his dad really is in the business, then maybe he's your ticket into the game."

I see my boy processing that information and his whole vibe changes.

"Yeah. Yeah. You may be right."

The speaker overhead squawks, and Ms. Callaway's voice booms into the gym. "ROMEO BLACKWELL, PLEASE REPORT TO THE PRINCIPAL'S OFFICE."

"Ooh." The kids all snicker and point at me.

I just roll my eyes at their silliness and then start to head out of the gym, but not before catching hold of Anjenai's glance. The connection is brief before she cuts her eyes away and gives me her back. The trek from the gym to the principal's office is a pretty long one, and the entire time I'm wondering why I've been called out of class. It could be anything, but I have a sinking feeling it's about the one thing I'm not ready to talk about.

When I enter the front office, Ms. Callaway glances up, pinches her lips together and shakes her head. A variety of kids are seated in a line of chairs against the wall. All of them, no doubt, are just waiting their turn to see the principal. Only I get the pleasure of being waved right through.

"She's expecting you," Ms. Callaway says, her voice heavy with disappointment.

Great. They all know.

I shuffle behind the counter and then knock one time on the principal's door before entering the office. "You wanted to see me, Aunt Thelma?"

Glancing up, she gives me a look that reminds me that I'm supposed to refer to her as Principal Vincent when we're on school property.

"Come on in here and shut the door," she says sternly.

No doubt about it. I'm in trouble. Quickly, I shut the door and plant my butt in the chair across the desk from her. For a few *long* seconds we just look at one another. After a while, I'm wondering if she asked to see me or if it was the other way around and I just forgot or something.

"You did call me out of class, right?"

My aunt pulls in a long breath and exhales even longer. "There's some rather disturbing gossip that's been brought to my attention."

My heart sinks.

"It's about you and Phoenix."

Now my gaze drops to the floor. More seconds tick by while the room fills with a deafening silence. She's going to have a long wait if she thinks I'm going to start talking first.

"Is it true?" she finally asks.

"What?"

"Don't play with me. Don't you *dare* play with me. You know exactly what I'm asking you about."

I squirm in my seat a little bit. "Phoenix is pregnant," I confirm. It is incredibly hard to spit the words out.

Aunt Thelma sucks in another long breath, but this time she stands up. "Have either one of you told your parents about this?"

"No, ma'am," I admit.

"Mind if I ask what on earth you're waiting for?" she snaps.

I glance at her again. "Right now I'm just trying to wrap my head around this. I mean, I just found out about this myself a couple of weeks ago." I watch my aunt as she pulls in several deep breaths.

"I ain't going to lie, Romeo. I'm extremely...extremely disappointed in both of you. I expected more from you two." She starts pacing. "Now, I'm not naive, and I'm not going to pretend I don't know that you kids are having sex. But I thought that you, especially, knew how to protect yourself."

My head hangs lower.

"Did you use any protection?"

I swallow hard, still uncomfortable about this subject. "No, ma'am."

Her pacing behind the desk speeds up. "What were you thinking? How could you be...?" She stops herself and shakes her head. "Is she going to keep the baby?"

"I think so. What? You think that she should get an abortion?"

"NO! I did not say that." She waves her finger at me.

"I'm just trying to find out whether you two have reviewed all your options. I want to know how you feel about this situation."

The question stumps me. "Truthfully?"

"Of course."

"Trapped." Ashamed that's how I feel, I quickly add, "I know keeping the baby is the right thing to do. This mistake isn't the baby's fault. But the way I see it is that we don't have that many options. I'm not killing my child."

"I understand and can respect that." She settles back into her chair. She still has this stunned look of disbelief. Maybe she hoped that I would come in here and laugh at the rumors instead of validating them. I wish I could have.

"Have you been to a clinic?" she asks.

"What for?"

"If you're sexually active, you need to know your status."

"What do you mean? I've only had sex with one girl."

"And how many men has she had sex with?"

"One!"

"Are you sure?"

I immediately think about how Phoenix loved to flirt with other guys in front of me in an attempt to make me jealous.

Aunt Thelma reaches for the phone.

"Whoa. Who are you calling?"

"Who do you think?"

"Wait a minute!" I leap out of my seat. "That's not part of your job."

"Excuse me?"

"We're not talking as aunt and nephew here. It's not your job to call my parents and inform them about something that has nothing to with my school life. It's personal and none of my *principal's* business. This is between Phoenix and me. We will talk to our parents when *we're* ready and not before." I've never talked to my aunt like this, and I can tell that she's more than a little surprised.

After another long and loud silence, she finally sets the phone back into the cradle. "All right, then. I'll respect your wishes on this."

"Thank you."

"But you will carry your butt down to the clinic and get yourself checked out."

That's something I can agree to. "Yes, ma'am."

She stands up again and walks around her desk. Before I know it, we're hugging each other. "Look. I just want you to know that I'm here if you need me. Your principal, your aunt—your friend. I'm always here if you need to talk. Okay?" She cocks her head.

"All right, Aunt Thelma." We hug it out again and exchange "I love you"s before I head back off to class.

seven

Anjenai—The New Guy

"Where the hell is Tyler?" I ask Nicole after Romeo runs out of the gym. She'd recently transferred into this class after deciding that choir wasn't for her.

She shrugs her shoulders and hardly spares me a look. "I don't know."

"What's wrong with you?" I ask, concerned.

"Nothing." Nicole shrugs again.

I'm not buying it. Something is obviously wrong. I take her by the arm and pull her aside. "Are you sure that you're all right? You look as if—"

"It's nothing." She tries to put on a smile but fails miserably. In fact, she looks like at any second she's going to burst out crying.

"Nicole."

"Really, Anjenai. It's nothing." She sniffs and wipes at her eyes. "Just forget about it. Okay?"

Reluctantly, I nod.

Coach Whittaker blows her whistle. "I want everyone to

give me twenty laps around the court. Once you're done, take a seat on the bleachers."

Everyone moans and gripes. A few girls are already pulling out doctor's excuses so they can sit out.

Coach Whittaker rolls her eyes and blows her whistle. "LINE UP!" She turns to the new guy, Kwan. "I know that you didn't bring a change of clothes, so you're excused and can sit this run out, if you'd like."

Kwan shrugs his shoulders and heads on over to the bleachers. I casually check out his profile. He's cute.

"What grade is he in?" I whisper to Nicole.

"I don't know. I think someone said that he was a sophomore," she says dispassionately, which causes me to frown at her again. I really wish that she would tell me what's bothering her, but if I'm learning anything this year it's how to stay in my lane. I'm not going to push. She'll talk to me when she's ready.

I steal another peek at the new guy and I'm momentarily thrown off my game when I find his gaze locked onto me, as well. He's actually really good-looking. Kind of reminds me of Trey Songz. Same complexion, pouty lips and mesmerizing brown eyes. And he can dress, too. His lines are so clean he looks like he is brand-new.

"I wonder where he's from," I whisper.

Nicole doesn't say anything. She's gone back to looking lost inside her own little world.

Coach Whittaker blows her whistle again, and everyone takes off running around the court.

With Nicole being so quiet, I find myself wondering

where Tyler is again. Is she really hanging out with Billie Grant's old crew? What kind of upside-down world am I living in? Then, like a bad habit, my thoughts drift back over to Romeo. Why was he called to the principal's office or, rather, his aunt's office? *Why the hell do I care?*

I suck in a deep breath and instruct myself to stop thinking about him. But that is easier said than done. Just being in this gym keeps bringing back so many memories of that extremely short time together. We dated a few weeks, and it's probably going to take months to get over him. On the second lap, I cast another look over at the bleachers, and Kwan is still watching me. At least, I think he is.

Beside me, Nicole starts to wheeze.

"Are you all right?"

She pulls in deep gulps of air while she struggles to keep up with me. I slow down to make it a little easier on her. But by the time we get to the fifth lap, she's just tuckered out.

"It's all right. You just need to pace yourself," I advise her while jogging in place.

Nicole bends over, as if the air is sweeter below her waist. "Go on," she pants. "I'll catch up."

"That's all right. I'll wait for you to catch your breath."

"I said go on," she snaps.

Surprised, I just blink at her. It's like watching a kitty cat turn into a ferocious lion. "All right. All right." I toss up my hands. "I don't need a brick building to fall on my head." By the time I make another lap, I pass Nicole taking her time walking. Not willing to risk getting my head bitten off a second time, I just breeze right on past her.

Coach Whittaker blasts her whistle again. "MS. DIX, PICK IT UP!"

Nicole ignores her and continues her slow stroll around the court.

Around the tenth lap, more girls join Nicole in getting their walk on. I quickly make my twenty and then rush over to get some water out of the fountain. By the time I make it over to the bleachers there's a crush of girls surrounding Kwan.

"So you're a rapper?" one of the girls asks.

I roll my eyes. Every boy over eight thinks his ass can rap.

"Yeah. I spit a little something."

Again I roll my eyes, though I'm curious to hear how his husky baritone will sound flowing. It's different—even a little sexy. The other girls ooh and aah and then try to get him to show off his skills. He acts like he isn't going to give them a little taste, but c'mon, that false modesty only works for, like, two seconds.

Off beat, what you know about it?
All heat, all street, my dough I be about it

My ears perk up as I recognize KRS-One lyrics. I'm impressed because it tells me he's more about substance than flash. Then he kicks into something I've never heard before.

Everything about you is perfect to me
Your personality and your body, oh, it feels right to me

Our eyes lock.

I hope that nothing ever comes between us
'Cuz this love is like nothing I experienced before

My skin starts to tingle. The girls sitting around him follow his line of vision and give me the stank eye. I finally force myself to turn away, but I can still feel his heavy gaze on me.

Nicole finally stumbles her way over to the bleachers next to me. She's panting so hard, I'm wondering if she needs medical attention. "I think I got a cramp," she complains. "It ain't right for her to have us running around here like this after a lunch period."

Coach Whittaker blows that loud-ass whistle again, and then she and her assistant, Coach Griffin, start calling out names to divide everyone into teams.

"Good God. Now what?" Nicole whines.

"Maybe we could ask if you can sit this out," I offer and then want to bite my own tongue out.

Nicole just ignores me altogether. I'm starting to wonder if I did or said something to her at lunch that I don't know about. In the end, she does get out of doing basketball drills, which basically consist of everyone taking turns dribbling around orange cones and then attempting a free throw into the basket. I actually do pretty well. Mainly because

Romeo used the same tactic during our one-on-one private lessons.

There I go thinking about him again.

I breeze through the exercise while Nicole flat out refuses to participate. Still, I make all but one basket. This fact continues to astound the coaches.

"Hey, shorty," Kwan shouts out to me when the class heads toward the lockers.

I stop and glance back over my shoulder.

"You got mad skills, girl," he says, walking up to me and kicking up a killer smile. I appreciate the praise, but I'm a little weary of boys right now.

"Thanks," I say and then start to head back off.

"Whoa. Whoa." He grasps my wrist. "I'm trying to find out how you learned to play ball like that."

I shrug. "Around." What's the point of mentioning Romeo's name?

"Well. I'm impressed," he says, smiling into my eyes.

What am I supposed to say to that? "All right. Thanks, I guess."

Just then Romeo jogs back into the gym and catches Kwan and me standing there talking alone. He freezes, and his stare quickly turns into a glare.

I can't help turning back toward Kwan, this time with a syrupy smile. "I'll catch you later."

Kwan winks. "I'm going to hold you to it."

I jog off toward the lockers, feeling pretty damn good.

eight

Kierra—Nobody's Fool

Every idiot knows that it just takes one time to get pregnant. Right?

Nicole's words keep circling around inside my head like a carousel. Given my track record of having bad luck, I shouldn't be surprised that my first, painful, and short-as-hell sexual experience could possibly turn me into Maynard Jackson High's next baby mama.

Deborah. I close my eyes and groan at the thought of having to tell my older sister, the one who doesn't even want to take care of McKenya and me, that I might be bringing another mouth into her apartment to feed. I might as well start looking for a cemetery plot now. Things at my place are so tense now that I'm afraid the smallest thing will set off an explosion that will land my little sister and me in foster care.

It's no secret in my neck of the woods that my sister is a stripper at the infamous Champagne Room. She works long nights and sleeps all day. For the past three years when I come home from school, I'm the one who cleans the apartment, cooks dinner and makes sure that McKenya does her homework. Deborah was not too thrilled when I told her I wanted to try out for the freshman cheerleading squad and only agreed to it when I assured her that I would still be able to handle my chores around the house so it didn't infringe on her beauty rest.

Maybe it would all be worth it if McKenya at least cut me some slack. But no. She seems equally determined to make my life more difficult by whining or just being flat out stubborn. It's like she doesn't care or truly believe that Deborah will ever follow through with her weekly, if not daily, threats to abandon us. I, on the other hand, believe Deborah.

After all, she did it once…and for a full week, two years ago. I was twelve and McKenya eight. I kept lying to my baby sister, telling her that Deb was just pulling a double or sleeping—whatever it took not to alarm her that we were on our own. I didn't even tell Anjenai and Tyler. I was too afraid that they would let it slip and it would get around to some do-gooder adult who would call Family and Children's Services.

When Deborah came back, I couldn't tell whether she was relieved or irritated that we were still there. She just went to her room and slept off whatever had her looking like a hot-ass mess. She never said where she was or why she hadn't been home in a week, and I was too terrified to ask. I just went out of my way to make sure that she didn't perceive us as being a burden on her. But that was impossible to do sometimes.

And now this.

Tears swell at the back of my eyes while a cloud of doom hovers above my head. I'm so into my private world that I'm not paying attention to where I'm going until I literally ram into someone standing by my locker. "Oops. Sorry." I finally look up. "Romeo."

He spreads on a wide smile and I quickly give him a look that says, *Don't even try it.*

"Hey, Kierra. You got a minute?"

"As a matter of fact, I don't." I give him the cold shoulder and proceed to twirl the combination to my locker.

"Look. I owe you a big apology for what went down that night at Shadiq's party."

"Uh-huh."

"I'm sorry."

"For which part?"

He blinks like he had expected this bullshit to go down smoothly.

"Yeah. Just what I thought." I return my attention to my lock.

"For all of it," he finally says. "I know you won't believe this, but I *really* did—do—care for Anjenai."

"You have a funny way of showing it."

"You're right. I was an asshole that night. I messed up. I realize that, but you got to understand that I just had a lot dumped on me at that moment and shit just spiraled out of control before I could wrap my brain around everything that was happening."

"Uh-huh." I jerk open my locker and try to hurry and exchange the books I need for my next class.

"I was wondering if you could do me a favor."

"Ha!" I cut a look at him. "I like your nerve."

He's quiet for a minute. "You're upset."

"Gee. You aren't a dumb as you look." I slam my locker shut.

He meets my hard gaze. "And I got a feeling it's more at Chris than it is at me."

Just like that, he sweeps the floor from under me. "What did you say?"

Romeo glances around to make sure no one is listening to our conversation before easing closer to me. "I know what happened between you two that night."

I suck in a startled gasp. "He told you?"

The truth is written all over his face, causing my brain to reel in astonishment and embarrassment. "What? Was he boasting about it or something? Did it give you and your boys a good laugh?"

Scalding hot tears rush down my face.

"No. No, nothing like that. Please, don't cry. I didn't mean to upset you."

"You don't mean to do a lot of things lately, do you?"

Suddenly, he looks like a deer caught in headlights. *Everybody always expects me to just be this bubbly personality all the time. It's about time that some of them realize that I have claws, too,* I think to myself.

"I really understand why you and that asshole are friends now. Birds of a feather flock together." I start to storm off when he reaches out and grabs me by my arm.

"Whoa. Wait a minute."

I jerk my arm away. "Don't. Touch. Me."

A few rubbernecks swivel in our direction.

"What the hell are y'all looking at?" I snap. They turn their heads away while I refocus my attention on Romeo. "You tell that asshole friend of yours that if I hear so much as *one* word from someone else about that night, I will hunt him down and I'll cut off that pencil dick that he's so proud of." I close the gap between us and stab a finger in the center of his chest. "You got that?"

"Kierra, please, calm down."

"And as for you. Stay away from Anjenai. You don't deserve her. You're better off with your own kind—snakes." I finally turn away from him and storm down the hallway with more tears stinging my eyes.

He told them. I can't believe that he told them.

I wipe tears from my eyes, but it doesn't do any good because they're pouring like a waterfall. I make a pit stop in the girls' bathroom, and wouldn't you know it, Bianca and Raven are in there holding court over their usual fan base. I can't believe that I ever thought that they were cool.

I stop dead in my tracks just when their gazes jump up to see who dares to enter their domain. Not wanting to deal with the extra headache, I pivot and storm back out.

"YEAH, YOU BETTER RUN!" Bianca's squeaky, high-pitched voice yells out.

I stop for two seconds and battle my inner Tyler. Finally, I just let the BS roll off my shoulders. The Redbones are definitely not worth my time. I march down to my next class, mopping my face clean the best I can. I have no idea how I forgot that Christopher Hunter was in my next class. He is already seated at his desk and laughing with a bunch of other knuckleheaded kids. For a fraction of a second, our eyes lock. I throw imaginary daggers straight at his peanut head. In retrospect, that should've been my first clue that he didn't have much to work with downstairs.

The bell rings and I scramble to my seat like everyone else. Anger and hatred continue to roll off me in waves. Honestly, I'm trying to decide whether he's worth catching a case over.

"Pssst!"

The teacher stands and starts going over something. Hell, he could be talking in Latin for all I know. I'm too hot to pay him any attention.

"Pssst!"

I glance around.

"Pssst!"

I glance to my left and see Chris trying to catch Fiona's attention so that he can pass her a note. She finally glances back and sees what he's trying to do. I fold my arms and watch this heifer steal another glance at the teacher before swinging her hand back and accepting Chris's folded note.

My jaw is clenched tight while she unfolds the paper and reads. Two seconds later, she is giggling like those hyenas in *The Lion King*. She glances back at Chris and he puckers his lips and tosses a wink at her.

No, this boy ain't doing this shit in front of me.

Fiona grabs her pencil and scribbles something down and then passes it back. I'm sick to my stomach just watching them. By now all I can do is just simmer in my seat. A few minutes later, Mr. Gills is called out of the classroom and we're left with the instruction to work out the problems written on the board while he's gone. Of course, the minute he leaves the room, most of the kids bounce out of their seats and start cliquing together.

Chris is immediately leaning all over Fiona's desk and running his weak game on her. She just giggles and laughs while her overly glossed lips spread from ear to ear. I try to pull my attention from them, but my gaze keeps boomeranging its way back over to them.

"Nah. Nah. I ain't got a girlfriend," I hear him say.

Before I know it, I'm jumping up out of my seat, snatching my gear and running up out of there before my eyes spring another leak and I embarrass myself. I refuse to give him that satisfaction.

nine

Anjenai—Ex-Boy to the Next Boy

where *in the hell is Tyler?* I can't imagine her skipping out on basketball practice. It's one of the few things she likes about this school. Frankly speaking, I think we're the strongest members of the team.

On cue, the assistant coach blows his whistle and instructs us on a few warm-up exercises. I take another glance around before doing a few stretches and then a couple of laps around the court.

"Hey!" Daniella, a six-foot thirteen-year-old, catches my attention before jogging up next to me. "Where's your girl at?"

"I don't know. I don't think I've seen her since this morning."

"Oh." She falls silent for a long stretch, and then she asks, "So, what do you think about being on the team so far?"

I shrug. "It's okay."

Again, she falls silent for a while, and I suspect that I'm being set up for something.

"Sooo are you still getting private lessons from Romeo?"

There it is. I cut my eyes over at her. "Look, if you came over here to pump some gossip out of me, then you're wasting your time."

"Damn! I was just asking you a question." She mean mugs me and then speeds up to start whispering loudly to the group of girls running ahead of me. I roll my eyes and keep my pace. I swear, the girls in this school are working my nerves.

Today's practice turns out to be no joke. Coach Whittaker works us so hard, my clothes are drenched in sweat and I have muscles talking to me in places I never knew existed. But I do think that I'm improving, if the smile on Coach Whittaker's face is anything to judge by. The awkwardness I once felt with the fundamentals is quickly fading away.

I'm starting to feel like a natural on the court and even reveling in my ability to be aggressive with the plays the coach calls out. Off court, people tend to dismiss me as the shy and geeky girl between Tyler and Kierra. There's a little truth to that. Though I do know how to open a can of whupass from time to time. I have to, judging by how many times I have to jump into some foolishness that Tyler is in the middle of.

But on the court it seems like I've been given some sort of pass that allows me to work out pent-up frustrations, which I happen to have a lot of lately. Running, shoulder bumping, trash-talking. I feel so good flying down the court that I attempt my first slam dunk. The exhilaration of flying through the air and then watching the ball whish through the net is just beautiful. In that one second, I feel like I'm on top of the world. My scrimmage team roars with applause.

Coach Whittaker blows her whistle, and when I look over my shoulder at her I see her entire face lit up.

"Way to go, Anjenai!" She tucks her clipboard under her arm and joins in the applause. "Excellent play. But I need you to open up and be aware of your teammates and pass the ball. Daniella was wide open. Some of the best plays are the safe plays."

Was she? Hell, I didn't even notice, I was so in my own zone. I take the praise/criticism in stride and remind myself to do better. All in all, it turns out to be a great practice. I just hate that Tyler missed it. My scrimmage team is still giving me high fives and pats of congratulations as we head toward the locker room. After a shower and change back into my school clothes, I head toward the football field where the freshman cheerleading squad is practicing.

I wave to Kierra just as she's detaching from the group. Since we don't exactly have anyone who can pick us up, on days we have practice we walk the long blocks down to the closest city bus and go through a long series of transfers to ride back to our side of town. "Hey, girl. You about ready to head out of here?"

"Yeah. You already hit the shower?" she asks, frowning.

"Had to. Sorry. But I'll wait for you while you take yours."

"Great. 'Cuz I'm not about to get on a city bus smelling all funkdafied."

Even though she laughs, I get the feeling that something isn't quite right. "Are you okay?" I ask.

"Huh? Yeah. I'm fine. Why do you ask?"

I get the sense that she's lying, but I shrug anyway. "No reason."

She flashes me another smile. "C'mon. Let's go."

When we turn to head back to the gym I almost plow straight into Kwan's chest. "Oh!"

He smiles. "Sorry if I frightened you."

I step back and smile myself. He really does look like Trey Songz. "It's all right. I just need to make sure I look where I'm going."

His tongue slides across his lips and my heart starts fluttering. I'm surprised by this sudden warming in my lower belly. Those droopy eyes and two dimples are really working for him. "You know, I don't think that I properly introduced myself today in class. The name is Kwan."

I glance over at Kierra, and she has a look that is clearly asking for the 411.

"I'm Anjenai," I finally say.

"Believe me, I know. I've been asking around about you."

"Oh, great. I'm sure that you got an earful." Kierra and I start walking back toward the gym, but to my surprise Kwan decides to walk along beside me.

"I got the basics and a lot of gossip, but I've never been one to put too much stock in gossip."

I nod and wonder where he's going with this.

"I saw that slam dunk you did during practice. You're on fire when you're on that court."

"Thanks," I say, sounding all shy. Why is this gorgeous guy talking to me?

Kierra jumps into the conversation. "Are you a basketball fan?"

"Yeah. Actually, I have an older brother in the NBA. He plays for the Spurs. Rodney Simmons. Have you ever heard of him?"

"Sorry. I don't know that much about—"

"What, you play basketball like that and you don't even watch the game?"

Now I feel like a complete idiot.

"Well. We'll have to rectify that. Outside of music, my family lives and breathes basketball. You and your girl should come out to my crib. Pre-season games start this week. We can make it a small viewing party."

Is this a date? "Well...I, um..."

"Don't worry," he says, leaning over. "I promise I don't bite. And like I said. You can bring your girl here."

"Girls," Kierra says. "There'll be a few of us. Is there a problem with that?"

"Nah. Nah. The more the merrier." He winks.

But it's his voice I can't seem to get enough of. It's smooth, deep and a little husky all at the same time.

"It's a date," Kierra answers for me, and I cut my eyes at her for her choice of words. She just shrugs and mouths the word, *"What?"*

"Good," Kwan says. "I look forward to it."

We stop walking just before entering the gym. At that time, I realize that he's really staring at me. That warm feeling in my stomach is now spreading up to my chest. There's just something about the way that he's looking at me that's turning my mind into mush. I'm completely thrown off guard because it's just been a couple of weeks since I suffered the biggest embarrassment of my entire life. I'm starting to think I'm fickle or something. How can this new guy be pushing the same buttons that Romeo used to push such a short time ago? What does that mean? And what does it say about me?

"There you are, Kwan!" Bianca bounces her way over to our private circle with a big circus smile that I wish I could just slap off her face. "I've been looking all over the place for you." Her gaze finally shifts over to me, and I return her fake smile with one of my own.

Bianca's nose twitches. "I thought I smelled something foul out here."

"Then close your mouth," Kierra and I snap back in unison.

Kwan snickers while Bianca gives us the stink eye.

"*Anyway*, Kwan. A few of us are heading over to the mall. You want to come?" She is practically slathering herself all over the boy's arm.

I think I'm going to be sick, watching her perfor- mance.

"Actually, I was just having a conversation with—"

"C'mon, Kierra," I say, tugging on her arm. "Let's go."

"Yeah. Why don't you do that," Bianca jumps in with her two cents. It's like she's not going to be happy until we slap what little black she has off of her.

Kierra gives me this "Are you crazy?" look, but I ignore it. I don't have any business trying to talk to some new guy when my heart is still aching over the crap the last one put me through.

Bianca also tugs on Kwan's arm. "It'll be a lot of fun and a good way for you to meet all the *right* people."

"I don't know," Kwan says, looking me dead in my eye. "I already think I'm meeting some pretty cool people." He smiles and I can't help smiling back.

I push Kierra through the gym's back door.

"Don't forget our date," he calls out to me.

Bianca's face reddens as Kwan finally allows her to pull him away.

"Giiiirrl. That boy got it bad for you," Kierra says as we march across the gym. "When in the hell did you meet him?"

"Today. He's new."

"Must be. I don't think I would have forgotten someone like that roaming the halls. Do you know who he looks like?"

"Yeah. Yeah." I try to shoo off all her inquiries. I'm too confused with what's going on with me and wondering if it's too soon to be jumping back out into the frying pan and risking getting burned.

Then again, Romeo certainly didn't waste any time getting back with Phoenix.

ten

Tyler—Misunderstood

"shoplifting? You have to be kidding me!" My dad rants and roars while he speeds down the highway.

Sitting in the passenger seat of his rusting black Dodge Intrepid, I try to block out most of what he's going on about and just watch the boring scenery as we make our way home.

"I don't understand," he continues. "I thought we were doing good. I thought we were finally—" He sucks in a long breath, and I roll my eyes because I know it's just his usual way of counting to ten. From the corner of my eye I see him grip the steering wheel tightly. "Just tell me what happened?"

I don't have an answer for him. Besides, I wasn't the one who shoplifted anything. That was Michelle and Trisha's stupid asses, but since I was with them my ass has to go down in flames, too. My life is filled with shit that isn't my fault. At this point, who cares?

At my silence, my father's jaw tightens. So what? He's

mad and disappointed in me. Now he has a little taste of what I feel about him. Misery loves company, right? I recognize all the emotions that are playing out on his face, and a small part of me wants to laugh in his face and ask him, "How does it feel?" Let's face it. My father has never understood where I'm coming from. He just wants me to be as little trouble as possible.

"So you have nothing to say for yourself. Is that it?"

Silence.

He hits the steering wheel with the palm of his hand and unleashes a string of curses that nearly sets my ears on fire. I guess now I know where I get my temper from.

"I swear I don't know what to do with you anymore," he spits.

"Why do you have to *do* anything?" I finally spit back.

"Yeah. You're right. I should just kick back and watch you just ruin your life! That's a good idea!"

"I think that you and Mom have already done a good job ruining my life, remember?" I fold my arms with a huff and recast my gaze back out the passenger side window.

"You can't keep using your mother and me as an excuse, Tyler. You're not the only kid whose parents have divorced. Look around. The world does not revolve around you."

"Oh, trust me. I know that," I snap.

"Do you? You sure don't act like it. These little prima-donna hissy fits say otherwise. You think if you just lash out that maybe you'll get your way? It doesn't work like that. Hell, even your best friends' parents aren't around. What makes you so damn special that you feel you can run around breaking the law? You think the judge is going to give a damn?"

Silence.

"Look, I get that it's hard. But it's time you learn that *life* is hard. Guess what? It's just going to keep on getting harder. People are going to keep disappointing you. More people are going to leave you. You need to learn how to deal, or life is going to deal with you. Period."

Silence.

He exhales another long breath and tries again. "Hell, I miss your mother, too, but you don't see me running out here knocking over liquor stores and doing whatever I damn well please because my heart is broken. C'mon. You're smarter than that."

There's no way I can stop these fat tears from burning my eyes and rolling down my face, so I don't even try.

He's shaking his head as he exits the highway. "You know how much money I've lost today because I had to leave the job and come and get you out of jail? *Jail!* I can't afford this shit!"

"Here we go. Work, work, work!"

"Yes, work! I know at fourteen you think that money grows on trees, but it doesn't. I just spent our rent money posting bail—or maybe you like the idea of us being homeless. Is that it?"

Silence.

"Take another *good* look around, Tyler. Whether you like it or not, money makes the world go around. Money pays the bills, puts clothes on your back and keeps you from going to sleep hungry. But I guess you don't appreciate that."

I roll my eyes and wish that he would just shut the hell up. But clearly my silence means he can just keep on ranting.

"Damn, Tyler. I can't do everything. I can't work, provide *and* sit on top of you to make sure that you're doing everything that you're supposed to do. That isn't fair, and you know it! SHOPLIFTING? SMOKING POT?" He hits the steering wheel again. "WHAT THE HELL IS GOING ON WITH YOU?"

My tears are falling so fast that I close my eyes in an attempt to block everything out. But that's impossible today.

"You've been in high school what—a little less than two months, and you're already a rebel without a cause?"

I feel him whipping the car into Oak Hill Apartments. A few seconds later, he pulls into his usual parking spot. I'm hopping out of the car before he even gets a chance to shut off the engine.

"Tyler!"

I ignore him and rush toward our apartment. I know that he's hot on my tail, and if it wasn't for me having to slow down and fiddle with the damn lock, I would've made it to my bedroom and slammed the door before he could catch up with me. Instead, he grabs me by the arm in the living room and forces me to spin back around.

"You hold on, little girl. We're not through with this discussion."

"What is there left to say? I'm an expensive, pain-in-the-ass kid. I get it."

"Why in the hell weren't you in school?"

"I left so I could *steal* and *smoke pot*. I thought that we'd already gone over this?"

My father steps so close to me that I can feel his fiery anger just roll off of him. "Don't. Try. Me. Tyler." His gaze stabs my own. "I'm not one of these little girls you're always trying to fight, so I suggest you watch that mouth of yours before you write a check your ass can't cash."

I snatch my arm back. "No, you're not. You're father of the year," I accuse him. "You're too concerned with your job to even notice that I'm alive."

"What the hell are you talking about?" He steps back and stares me down. "What? You want attention? Is that what this is all about? Your getting locked up is some desperate cry for my attention?"

I shake my head at him. He doesn't get it. He won't get it. "Just forget it." I start to turn away, but once again, I'm forced to turn back around.

"We're not finished talking, young lady." He then proceeds to pull in several deep breaths, trying to calm down, but at this point I don't think that's really possible for either one of us. "I'm trying to talk to you. I've *been* trying to talk to you, but all you give me is either the silent treatment or snappy one-liners. I can't tell if you're trying to be a mute or a comedian."

"You're not talking to me, you're yelling at me!"

"I think under the current circumstances that I have the right to yell, Tyler! You're doing things I don't understand. Make me understand what's going on with you!"

I do understand his frustration but I can't explain something that I don't understand myself. My emotions are all over the map. At least I know that much. I'm angry all the time, and I don't know what to do about it.

"Talk to me, Tyler."

How? How can I talk to him about this huge hole my mother's leaving left in my heart without sounding like some whining baby who doesn't know how to deal with life? Instead of time healing all wounds, it seems like they're just sitting there festering into some incurable disease that's eating me alive.

While these thoughts race around in my head, my father's shoulders collapse in the face of what he undeniably sees as another dose of the silent treatment. He shakes his head.

"So what am I supposed to do now? Huh?" He cocks his head. "Should I get a *babysitter* to watch you in the evenings? Do I need each teacher at that school to call me if you don't show up for class?"

"You do what you have to do," I say with a smirk.

"I have to do *something.* You have a court date now. You might have to go to juvenile hall. Have you thought about that? Once you're in that system it's all downhill."

"At least I'll be out of your hair. You can work all the hours your heart desires then."

He stares at me. "I think you need help. Professional help."

"Can we *afford* that?"

His eyes narrow while a small vein begins to twitch on his right temple. He starts pacing. "I swear I don't know what to do with you."

"I think we've already covered that."

"I don't know how she did it. I don't know how your mother put up with you."

The mere mention of my mother causes my heart to jump, but there's an underlying insinuation that *I* was the reason behind her leaving. I can't help gasping and step back at him. "It's you," I accused him. "It's *your* fault she left. And you know what? I don't blame her. I can't stand you, either!" I grab a glass vase with dusty, fake flowers in it and hurl it at his head.

He just barely ducks out of the way. "What the hell?" He charges toward me, jerking his hand back, but then it suspends in the air as if some invisible force is holding him back from slapping me into the middle of next week.

"What? You want to hit me? Just like you used to hit Mom?"

My words are like a weapon of mass destruction judging by the complete devastation across his face. He lowers his hand and takes another step back away from me.

"I HATE YOU!" I scream and then take off running to my room, sobbing so hard that I can't even see straight. My door slams like a bolt of thunder hitting the small apartment. No doubt everyone in the building heard it, but I don't care. I lock the door and then hurl myself across the bed and cry into my pillow.

eleven

what *the hell was I thinking?*

I pull in several deep breaths and then pace around in a circle. I have half a mind to storm back to Tyler's bedroom and remove the hinges off that damn door. Who in the hell does she think she is talking to me like that? I'm trying to calm down, but it's hard. *I hate you!* Those words are ringing in my head. Mainly because those are the exact same words Victoria shouted at me countless times.

"What? You want to hit me? Just like you used to hit Mom?"

She got that shit backwards. It was Victoria who used to do all the throwing and hitting. I don't know what the hell she's talking about. I was the one doing all the ducking and diving just like I was doing a few minutes ago. Tyler definitely has her mother's temper.

I know I need to try and finish this argument, but what else can I say? I'm not getting through to the girl. That's just a fact. I know it may sound jacked up, but for the gazillionth time I found myself wishing that Tyler was a boy. Boys are easier to deal with. They mess up, you just pop them on the back of the head one good time. When your little girl messes up, it's like your heart is being scooped out of your chest with a jagged spoon.

You insinuated that her mother left because of her. No. I didn't. *Yes, you did.* My mind hit an instant replay button and I hear myself saying, *"I don't know how she did it. I don't know how your mother put up with you."*

After hearing that, I start groaning under my breath. Damn, I'm starting to wonder if I'm causing just as much psychological and emotional damage to the girl as her mother did and I'm the one who stuck around.

Music suddenly blares from Tyler's bedroom. It's so loud it sounds like Jay-Z is performing in the apartment. A part of me wants to storm back there and demand that she turn that racket down, but another part remembers the days when I used to pull that same tired stunt on my own parents. She just needs to vent better with music than with throwing things at my head again. My daughter has a good arm on her.

I continue pacing around the living room, remembering how scared I was to receive that call from her from jail. *Jail!* I still can't get over it. How did I get here? I never imagined that I would be the kind of father who had to deal with a child who went to jail. That sort of thing happens to other people's children—not my own.

I shake my head, suddenly needing something to drink— something strong. Swiveling around, I storm out the door and give it a good, hard slam myself. The only problem is that Ms. Maureen, Anjenai's grandmother, is stepping out of my neighbor's door, and she gives me a look that questions my sanity.

I clear my throat. "Sorry about that," I say, embarrassed, and then quickly storm off.

Back in the car, I peel out of the apartment parking lot like a bat out of hell. However, I don't have any idea where I'm going. Sure, I needed a drink, but tangling with alcohol right now would not be such a good idea. I just need space. *We* need space.

Ten minutes later, I end up at the Waffle House. It's a small diner that's just slightly better than a truck stop. Most people come for the grease and not necessarily the food. Just seconds after walking into the brightly lit, square-shaped diner, I spot Deborah sitting in a corner booth. I ain't going to lie, just that cursory glance at her has brightened my day. I walk up to the breakfast counter and pop a squat on one of the small, round stools. All the while, I keep one eye trained on my beautiful neighbor. And I'm not the only one. Every dude up in here is peeping her out and probably trying to work up the courage to approach her.

Hands down, Deborah Combs is a stunningly beautiful woman. It's no secret in this neighborhood that she's the main attraction down at the Champagne Room. From time to time our paths have crossed, but not as much as one would think since one of her sisters is one of Tyler's best friends. *At least she was spared being called down to the police station.*

I remember when Deborah first took in Kierra and McKenya, about three years ago. Actually, the Combses' situation made all the city papers. Michelle Combs, whom I used to think I knew pretty well, was sent upstate for killing her husband, Kenneth Combs. Now, I didn't really know Kenneth all that well, but what I did know of him, I didn't like. I think it was the way Michelle took out her husband that surprised many of us who followed the trial. There was no screaming or hollering. No guns or artillery. She simply cooked him a feast of all his favorite soul food and laced it with some type of poison that I don't remember offhand. He died while sucking on some ribs.

Pretty cold-blooded.

If I remember correctly, Michelle Combs never gave a motive, and therefore she was sentenced to life in prison without the chance of parole.

Deborah seemed supportive at first, but then I think the stress of being so young and now being responsible for her two sisters is weighing down on her. I can easily relate, and I have just *one* child to deal with.

"What can I get you?" my waitress suddenly pops up at the counter to ask.

Hell, I haven't even looked at the lunch menu. Reluctantly, I pull my gaze away from Deborah and pick up the plastic menu. "Just, um, get me the number one with a Coke."

"How would you like your burger?" she asks, not bothering to hide how bored she is.

"Well done."

"All right. Coming right up." She turns and yells my order to the guy working the grill, even though he's just two feet from her.

I steal another peek over toward Deborah's booth, but

this time my gaze crashes right into hers. I try to pass it off with a nod and a polite smile.

"Care to join me?" she asks, loudly.

Every man's head swivels in my direction. "Don't mind if I do." I climb back off of my stool and catch my waitress's attention. "I'm moving over to the corner booth." By the time I slide into the empty space across from Deborah, I have to admit that I'm a bundle of nerves. "I didn't know that you like to hang out at the Waffle House."

"I don't," she admits. "But I just needed to get out of that apartment for a while. I was beginning to think that the walls were closing in on me, you know?"

I bob my head while picking up the scent of vanilla clinging to her skin. "I know *exactly* what you mean."

We fall into a comfortable silence, and I think her thoughts drift for a moment. When her gaze finds mine again, I think she just then remembers that I'm even sitting there.

"So how's the whole single-father thing going for you?"

I shake my head while my frustrations with my daughter start inching my blood pressure up a few notches. "I think the safe answer is 'I'm still standing.'"

"Good." She flashes me that beautiful smile. "That makes two of us."

"Then things aren't going too well?" I inquire.

Deborah's warm, coffee-colored eyes drift off again. "It's just a lot harder than I anticipated. I mean I knew that it would be hard, you know. Taking care of a thirteen- and a nine-year-old is not for the faint of heart. I'm not naive.

I used to be those ages, but—" She starts shaking her head again. "It just feels like no matter what I do, it's never quite enough. Those girls have no idea what it's like to work to pay the bills. But working double shifts means sleeping when they're awake and working when they're sleeping. And the few times that I do manage to be conscious, I'm so bone tired and frustrated, and I just feel so—"

"Unappreciated?"

Her smile stretches wider, and two dimples wink at me. "You *do* understand."

"More than you'll ever know."

She nods, but her smile is fading fast. "I don't know if I'm doing such a hot job. I snap when I don't mean to and say things that I don't mean and I've done some things that I regret."

"Hmm."

"Hmm, what?"

"Hmm. I'm starting to think that you have my apartment bugged."

She laughs, and I'm enjoying its rich sound. I take a few seconds to drink in her strong profile: her small, heart-shaped face, her long hair and those mesmerizing lips. She doesn't have on that much makeup from what I can tell, and she's still just as gorgeous as the few times I've seen her leaving for work all decked out.

Suddenly, I start wondering if she has a boyfriend. A while back I'd asked her out for pizza, but I don't know whether she considered it a serious offer. Looking at her, I can't see how she wouldn't have a boyfriend. Still, I've never seen any guys hanging around or her bringing anyone home—then again, I'm not always around myself.

"My mother lost her appeal today," she says.

The change in topic throws me off guard a bit. "I'm sorry to hear that." I watch so many emotions ripple across her face, all of them slowly breaking my heart.

She sniffs and wipes away a tear. "I don't know how much longer I can do this," she admits, reaching for her coffee. "Sometimes I think that Kierra and McKenya would have been better off if they had been placed in foster care."

"You don't mean that," I tell her.

Silence.

I draw in a deep breath. "Are things *that* bad?"

Her eyes fill with more tears. "I'm not good with children," she says. "I never have been. I mean, I've got my own set of problems, you know?"

I bob my head, but I'm put off a bit by the notion that an adult really thinks she has the option of walking away from her responsibilities. My waitress shows up and plops my lunch down on the table in front of me. "Thank you," I mumble to the waitress.

"Can I get you anything else?" she asks, chewing the hell out of a wad of bubble gum.

"No, thanks. That will be all." When I glance back over at Deborah, I notice that her shoulders are slumping lower by the second.

"Can I tell you something?" she whispers, swiping the corners of her eyes.

"Sure."

She pauses for a moment, but then starts talking in a low

whisper. "When I first got the call about my mother's arrest, I was actually thrilled. She'd finally done it. She had finally taken a stand against that bully."

Now I'm just stunned speechless, but I sit and listen.

"That son of a bitch made my life miserable. I never thought she'd find the backbone to stand up to him. And when she did…well, let's just say that he never saw it coming. But the repercussions, I don't think either of us really thought about what those might be. Now it just all seems like too much." She sniffs again and wipes at her eyes. "At first I thought I could do it. They would be a lot better off with me than growing up in that house with *that* man. His temper and the things he did when he thought that no one was looking." She shakes her head. "I thought that—" She swallows and then falls silent for so long that I don't think that she's going to finish the sentence.

Even though I want to comfort her, I'm not sure how to go about doing that. She's talking about turning her sisters over to foster care to break up her family just because life is hard. Sure, I feel inadequate when it comes to dealing with Tyler but leave? Never.

"You know what? I gotta go."

She grabs her purse, and I see my window of opportunity to help her closing.

"McKenya is going to be home soon, and I think Kierra is still at cheerleading practice."

She fumbles with her purse so badly that she tilts it the wrong way and half the contents spill out of it. "Goddamn it!"

"Here, let me help you," I say.

She's a nervous flutter of movement while she shoves things back into her purse. I reach over as well and then stop cold when I see a small vial of white powder. "Hey, that's mine." She snatches it out of my hands and shoves it into her purse.

"I—I'm sorry. I didn't mean—"

"I'll catch up with you later," she says, flying from the booth and racing out of the diner so fast that she looks like a blur.

I'm left sitting there wondering what the hell just happened.

BFF Rule #9

Remain loyal through good times and bad.

twelve

Phoenix—The Bitch is Back

Things are changing. I know this because Bianca and Raven, my two supposed best friends, aren't waiting for me by my locker before the homeroom bell. The reason this is significant is that we've always met up at my locker since we were in junior high. But I'm not going to completely freak out, because lately I have been missing a lot of days. Don't get me wrong. I know these girls think that because I'm pregnant or was pregnant they are clear to try to take my shine. Silly rabbits, tricks are for kids. I'm always going to be the number-one diva.

I quickly jerk open my locker and pull out what I need before checking my reflection in the mirror glued to my locker door. Behind me I see a few girls snickering and whispering, so I turn around and flash them all the bird. They gasp at having been caught and then quickly get out of my face with all that nonsense. These chicks got the wrong idea if they think that they can run a shame campaign on me. I don't play that crap.

Sure, when I slam my locker shut and make my way toward my homeroom I can feel just about every eye swivel toward me. But I keep my chin up and a smile on my face. Haters. Each and every one of them.

I reach my homeroom a couple of minutes before the bell and apparently catch my homeroom teacher, Ms. Hopkins, by surprise because she looks up from her desk with an overly sunny greeting. "Ooooh, Phoenix. I'm so happy to see that you're back today. How are you feeling?"

All the kids in the classroom stop what they're doing and turn to see how I'll answer. Clearly the gossip has finally worked itself up to the teaching staff.

"I'm doing great. Thanks for asking." I give her a plastic smile and then make my way over to my desk at the back of the room while everyone starts whispering again. A few seconds later, Bianca and Raven giggle their way into the classroom and then stop cold when they spot me in the back.

"Close your mouths. You're letting flies in," I tell them.

"Phoenix, you're back," Bianca squeaks and then runs her gaze over me as if trying to see whether I'm showing yet.

Raven's smile turns into a slow smirk as she makes her way over to my desk. "Well, I'm glad to see that you're back. This place is never the same when you're gone."

I roll my eyes at my little Puerto Rican ass kisser.

"Had we known that you were coming to school today we would've met you at your locker."

"Check your text messages," I tell them.

"Oh." Bianca whips her phone out, reads and then gives me an apologetic smile. "Our bad. Forgive us?"

"Yeah. Whatever." I grab my purse and pull out my compact and lip gloss. Romeo should be here any minute now. "So what have you two bitches been up to?"

"Giiirrl," Bianca says, dropping into the desk in front of me. "There's this new guy here at the school who is fiiiine."

"Capital F–I–N–E," Raven co-signs.

"Oh, really?" I ask, puckering my lips at my mirror.

Bianca pushes my mirror down. "No. You don't understand. I'm talking Romeo finally has some competition as being the finest brother in this school."

"I know I wouldn't mind him being my baby daddy," Raven says, chuckling.

Both Bianca and I cut her with a look.

"What? Oh." At least she has the common decency to look embarrassed. "Sorry."

I roll my eyes again.

"Anyway," Bianca continues, "I got my eye on Kwan. That's his name, by the way. Give me one week and I'll be wearing his class ring."

"Oh, I like your nerve."

"Girl, chill out. You still have Chris sniffing behind you."

"Please. Chris ain't nothing but a baby player trying to rub up on anyone that'll have him. I'm not stuttin' him, and that weak-ass game he spits all the time."

"Too bad, Kwan's mine. You can have Shadiq."

"What? This boy has been in this school for one day and you two are already fighting over him?"

"Wait until you see him," they chime together.

Now I'm a little curious.

"I can't wait to show up at homecoming with him on my arm," Bianca sighs like a Disney princess. "I'm sure that we'll be a shoo-in for homecoming king and queen."

I clear my throat. "I think that'll be me and Romeo."

"Yeah. I'm sure that maternity dresses will be all the rage," she jabs.

"Please." I fold my arms. "I can roll through there nine months pregnant with elephant feet and still outshine you two bitches, so stay in your lane." I check Bianca's fast mouth with a hard stare and dare her ass to say something else smart back to me.

Romeo strolls into the room laughing with Shadiq. I glance up and smile over at him. He doesn't smile back. In fact, he just draws in a deep breath and looks like I'm the last person he wanted to see this morning. That is definitely not a good sign.

Our homeroom classes allow us to sit anywhere we want. And usually Romeo and his crew sit in the back with the Redbones. So how come this boy pops a squat into one of the vacant desks in the *middle* of the class? I blink in surprise at the open diss. My girls share a look and then glance back at me to see what I'm going to do about the situation. Soon after, the rest of the class starts whispering and snickering.

The hairs on the back of my neck stand straight up, and my face is so hot it feels like it's on fire. The morning bell rings and Ms. Hopkins pops up out of her seat to start roll call.

I sit and simmer until she finishes, and then afterward we have about fifteen minutes to study or pray or take a nap. I, of course, spring up out of my seat and make my way over to Romeo's desk.

"Mind if I talk to you for a minute?" I ask and pretend that all eyes aren't on us.

Again, Romeo gives me this look like he doesn't want to be bothered.

"Please," I add with a low hiss that lets him know we can do this quietly or at the top of my damn voice.

He finally pushes out of his chair and then follows me to a corner of the room. "Yeah. What's up?"

"I think I need to be asking, what's up with you?"

"Nothing."

It's a bad lie and we both know it. I cock my head at him. "You want to try that again?"

He sighs and rocks his head from side to side while he licks his lips. "Look, I've been thinking."

"Thinking?" I fold my arms. "Well, this should be good."

"Look. I understand that you're pregnant."

I look away from him.

"And I'm going to be a father to my child. It's just that me and you—"

"What?"

"We don't work anymore. We're not a good fit. And we haven't been for some time now."

My heart stops and drops down to my toes. "What do you mean?"

"C'mon. You know exactly what I mean, Phoenix." He draws in another breath. "Now, I admit that this whole situation threw me for a loop, and it took me a minute to try and clear my head, but after talking to my aunt yesterday, I think I've made some decisions."

"Your aunt?"

"Shhh. Keep your voice down."

I grind my teeth. "Your *aunt* is not the one who knocked me up. You did." I stab him in the chest with my finger. "Therefore, she doesn't have any say in the matter."

He refuses to look me in my eyes.

"What? She told you to leave me? Did she tell you to let me do this shit on my own, is that what you're telling me?"

"No. She didn't say anything like that."

"Oh. Well, she said something. Because a couple of days ago we were in this together."

"She was just asking me how I *felt* about things. You know, something that you never did ask me. You've been making all the decisions from the giddy up. From whether to keep the baby to us walking down the aisle."

"Whether to keep... Did she suggest that I have an *abortion?*"

"NO!" Romeo glances around and then lowers his voice. "She just got me to see that just because we made one mistake there's no need for us to make another by trying to stay together."

"Let me tell you something, Romeo. I didn't get into this

mess by myself, and I'll be damned if I just let you turn me into some pathetic baby mama while you're free to go off and party hearty through your high-school years like you don't have a care in the world. Knowing you, you got your mind fixed on chasing after that hood rat Anjenai."

Guilt flushes his face.

"Naw. It ain't going down like that. It's me and you like it's always been and how it will always be. So get your mind out of the clouds and focus on your responsibilities!" It isn't until I turn around that I see that everyone is straining the hell out of their necks trying to put their noses in our business. "What the hell are y'all looking at?" I snap. I rush over to my desk, grab my things and storm toward the door.

"Ms. Wilder, where do you think you're going?" Ms. Hopkins calls out.

I don't pay her any mind as I race out of the room. I'm a hurricane of fury as I make my way to the front office.

"I need to speak with Principal Vincent," I thunder at Ms. Callaway.

There's a line of kids sitting in plastic chairs, but I'm not about to wait to say what's on my mind.

"Wait, Phoenix!"

Wait, hell. I shove the door open and announce, "We need to talk!"

Principal Vincent and Vice Principal Palmer spring away from each other so fast it's damn near comical.

"Sorry, Thelma. She breezed right past me."

"Hmm, huh." I jab my hands on my hips and tap my foot. "I guess the rumors are true."

Principal Vincent's eyes narrow on me as she settles her own hands on her hips. "Thank you, Ellen. I've got this."

I glance back over my shoulder, and Ms. Callaway gives me the stank eye as she shrinks back out of the office, closing the door behind her.

"Ms. Wilder, I do believe you know not to just barge into my office like that."

"I do believe that you know to keep your nose out of my *personal* business."

Mr. Palmer steps forward. "Check your tone, Ms. Wilder."

"What part of personal business don't *you* understand, Mr. Palmer?"

Fire leaps into this man's eyes, but I hold my own. I don't give a rat's ass if I hurt his girlfriend's feelings. She needs to keep her nose out of my business.

"Mr. Palmer, can you excuse us for a few minutes?" *Thelma* asks.

He hesitates, but I simply lift my brow as if to ask what the hell he is waiting for. Finally, he backs off.

"Call me if you need anything," he tells Thelma and then slowly strolls out of the office.

"Now. What seems to be your problem, Ms. Wilder?" she asks, folding her arms.

"I'm talking to Romeo's *aunt*. You know, the one who was just free to give advice on something that doesn't concern her. The one who thinks it's her place to suggest that I get an abortion!"

"I did no such thing!"

"Well, that's how I'm going to tell it to my parents, the

school board and then all those lovely people down at the local news stations if you don't back the hell up and stay in your lane."

The color drains out of Thelma's face.

"You think I'm playing? Do you really want to call my bluff? Try me. If I lose Romeo over your big mouth, I'm going to make damn sure you'll never find another job as a principal again."

Silence.

"Are we clear?" I challenge her. I stand there glaring back at her so that she knows that I'm not playing. Abortion is a hot potato here in the South, and the last thing she wants to do is stir up the Bible Belt's Christian soldiers. "Good," I say after taking her silence as a clear understanding. "You have a good day today." I wink, turn and stroll out of the office with my head held high.

thirteen

Kierra—The Longest Two Minutes

MY period is three days late. I'm trying not to let that fact worry me, but it's hard. All I can think about is my stomach getting big, my feet swelling, and stretch marks. I've heard that once you get stretch marks they never go away. One thing for sure is that I can't tell Deborah. Yet I'm such a small person, I don't know how I'm going to hide it. Maybe if I start wearing bulky clothes now, by the time I start to show no one will get suspicious. Of course, if I am pregnant I will have to tell my girls what happened between Chris and me at that party. I'm not sure if I'm ready to do that.

I know that keeping secrets is against the BFF rules, and it was secrets that caused problems at the beginning of the school year, but this is different. What happened between Chris and me that night is too humiliating to even put into words. I just want to forget that it ever happened. Now that's going to be difficult to do if I have a baby baking in my oven.

There's a Rite Aid pharmacy two blocks from our

apartments. The place is like my second home, because I usually get all my makeup and fashion magazines from there. Today I'm going to pick up a pregnancy test. I tell Deborah I just need to go for some tampons, and she makes me take McKenya with me. *Just great.*

McKenya is just as thrilled about going as I am about taking her. There are three things my little sister doesn't like to do: wake up in the morning, be pulled away from her cartoons, and do her chores. And right now I'm interrupting her *SpongeBob* marathon.

"I don't see why I have to go!"

"That makes two of us," I snap.

"Why can't you go to the store tomorrow?"

"What difference does it make? SpongeBob is on every day. Today, tomorrow, Deborah is still going to make you walk to the store with me. So we might as well go ahead and get it over with."

McKenya stomps toward the door. "Let's hurry up. Maybe we can make it back before the cartoons go off."

"Go get your sweater," I tell her.

Deborah emerges from her bedroom decked out from head to toe in leather. I'd be lying if I said that she didn't look good. She does. She always looks good. But once again she is running late for work and rushing through the apartment like a wild hurricane.

"You look pretty, Deb," McKenya says.

"Thanks, honey."

"Do you think you could just give us a ride to the pharmacy? We can walk back," I say.

Deborah glances at her watch and makes a face. "Oh, I don't know…"

"Never mind. McKenya, I told you to get your sweater."

My older sister huffs out a long breath. "All right. Y'all just hurry up and get in the car."

"Yea!" McKenya jumps up and down, mainly because she thinks she's going to get back to SpongeBob faster.

Whatever. I just rush out to the car before she changes her mind—not that riding in my sister's junky black Celica is some kind of luxury ride. It isn't. In fact, I don't think she has ever cleaned this puppy out. Not to mention that there have been plenty of times when she has forgotten to roll her windows up before a storm, and the interior has mildewed a thousand times over. Despite that I hold my breath and climb into the backseat. McKenya jumps into the front passenger seat and buckles up.

Deborah slides in behind the wheel and starts the engine before closing the door. "Kierra, do you have your house keys?"

I quickly check my pockets in here and my keys jingle. "Yeah, got them."

Deborah slams her door and peels out of her parking space like a bat out of hell. The Rite Aid is not on her way to work, but it's just two blocks. She screeches to a stop in front of the pharmacy and then orders us to hurry out of her car. I just barely get the door slammed before she's rocketing off to work. Shaking my head at the exhaust smoke coming out of her tailpipe, I grab McKenya's hand and head on into the pharmacy.

"Can I get a chocolate bar?" McKenya asks.

"I don't care."

My sister races off to the candy aisle while I head toward the back on the hunt for a pregnancy test. Wouldn't you know it, there are like a million people milling around in front of the body lubricants, condoms and pregnancy tests. I don't really want to draw any attention, but it seems like all eyes are on me when I inch toward the First Response and Clearblue pregnancy tests. I guess the best thing to do in this situation is just thrust up your chin and act like you know what you're doing.

I grab the first box I come to and nearly choke on the price tag. "Twenty dollars? They have to be kidding." I look back now on the shelf and try to find the cheapest test they have. I quickly find a generic store brand that is about eight bucks cheaper and decide to go with that one. I glance back up. I get a lot of smirking looks, but I just wrinkle my nose at them and then go on about my business. Head on over to the candy aisle to get McKenya, but she's not there. "Now where is she?"

Looking around, I try to spot a short person in a pink sweater. I still don't see her. "McKenya!" I start roaming up and down the aisles calling her name. She doesn't answer back, and I still can't find her. My heart drops out of my chest and my brain starts to fry. *Oh, my God! What if someone snatched her?*

"McKENYA!" I'm twirling around in a panic. "Has anybody seen my little sister? She's about four foot seven and wearing a pink sweater!" I rush from one person to another. They all are shaking their heads at me. "Somebody has to have seen her! McKENYA!"

I race back to the candy aisle, hoping that she will materialize. No such luck. I race out the front door and glance around the parking lot. "McKENYA!" Oh, God. What am I going to do? What am I going to tell Deborah? She's definitely going to kill me when I tell her I lost our little sister.

"Excuse me, ma'am? But is this who you're looking for?" Standing next to a woman in a Rite Aid smock, McKenya is frowning up at me. I nearly collapse with relief.

"McKenya. Where were you? Didn't you hear me call your name?" I rush over and throw my arms around her. "Don't you ever scare me like that again!" And I hug her tighter.

"I had to use the bathroom," she says meekly.

I didn't check the bathrooms. I wipe the tears streaming from my face. "From now on, when we come to the store you don't leave my side. You understand me?"

"Okay."

I grab her by the hand and lead her back into the store so I can pay for my pregnancy test, and I even buy her two candy bars. As we march back home I damn near have a death grip on McKenya's hand, but she doesn't utter a single complaint. I think she knows just how much she scared me, and neither one of us finds it funny. When we reach the apartment she still has about thirty minutes of *SpongeBob* left. She quickly plants herself back in front of the TV, and I march back toward the bathroom.

"Aren't you going to start dinner?"

"Yeah. Just give me a few minutes."

She makes a face but again she doesn't say anything.

Maybe I'll have a whole evening without her complaining. In the bathroom, I shut and lock the door before tearing into my generic pregnancy test. I read the instructions four times before hopping on the toilet. A few minutes later, I'm pacing back and forth waiting for the results to show up on the stick.

"Please don't let me be pregnant, God. *Please*. I swear that from here on out I'll be a good girl. I make all *A*s. I'll keep the apartment clean. And I will stay away from boys. Wait. Maybe that last one will be a little hard to do, but I'll try to stay away from bad boys."

I glance at my watch. Time's up. I reach for the pregnancy test and read my results.

fourteen

Anjenai—We Are Family

"shoplifting? Are you sure?" I ask Granny. I'm totally taken by surprise by this latest revelation. Tyler hasn't been in school for the past couple of days, and I assumed that she was sick. However, when I went to check on her no one would come to the door. So when Granny drops this news on me at the dinner table I'm left sitting here with my mouth open in shock.

"Yes, I'm sure. I got word from Ms. Todd—Michelle Todd's mother. Michelle, Tyler and some girl named Trisha were arrested at a strip mall not too far from the school. I know I saw Leon hot under the collar a couple days ago. I gather that he wasn't too happy having to take time off from work to go bail her out of jail."

"How come you didn't go to jail with Tyler?" Gregory, one of my ten-year-old twin brothers, asks me with a mouth full of macaroni and cheese.

"Now, what did I tell you about talking with your

mouth full?" Granny scolds, but with a soft smile hugging her lips.

"Sorry, Granny," Gregory mumbles, again with a full mouth.

"Besides, Anjenai knows better than to get herself tangled up in some shoplifting scheme. Don't you, Anje?" Granny levels a look at me that's all the warning I need.

"Yes, ma'am."

"Uh-huh." She keeps her eyes leveled on me to make sure that we have an understanding that she is not going to tolerate any foolishness.

In my mind she really doesn't have to worry, because I would never get involved in something like that. When it comes to Tyler I'm surprised but not surprised at the same time. Tyler has been on a self-destructive path for some time now, and clearly things are just getting worse. Michelle Todd, that's that girl who used to hang around Billie Grant. The same girl whose nose we broke on the first day of school. So what Kierra told me at lunch the other day is true.

I shake my head and wonder again what Tyler must be thinking. It's no use because I have no idea. And something tells me that Tyler doesn't, either.

"How come you don't talk about your boyfriend anymore?" Edafe, my six-year-old brother, asks, reaching for his Kool-Aid.

"I've never talked to you about any boyfriend," I remind him. "You were just always putting your nose in my business."

"It's everybody's business when you're playing kissy face

in his car in front of the apartment so the whole world can see," Hosea, the eight-year-old, chimes in.

The problem with living with four younger brothers is that they are always trying to eat into my business—what little I have. And they always seem to think that my life is an excellent topic of conversation for the dinner table.

"You boys leave your sister alone," Granny pipes up and then steals a peek at me to check if I am okay. After that disastrous party at Shadiq's a few weeks ago, Granny was alarmed when I came home sobbing my eyes out. I told her the whole story about how Romeo had embarrassed and abandoned me in the middle of our date to go crawling back to his ex-girlfriend. I didn't bother telling her about the pregnancy part because that would just alarm her about who was and who wasn't having sex. That's one big headache I would prefer to avoid.

"Do you mind if I run over to Tyler's after dinner?"

Granny doesn't look too pleased with that idea. I know that she's already wondering if Tyler is going to start becoming a bad influence on me.

"Come on, Granny. It's Tyler. I need to find out what's going on with her. She hasn't been acting like herself lately, and I'm concerned." Expressing concern is a shoo-in to getting her to let me go. No way Granny would suggest that I abandon a friend in need.

"Well...I guess you can run over there for a little while."

"Thanks, Gran." I quickly start shoveling the rest of my dinner into my mouth.

"Slow down. You're going to choke."

I cram in the last bite of meat loaf and then hop up from the table, taking my plate and glass to the kitchen sink. "I'll be back in a few," I tell everyone at the table and run out of the apartment. My mind is still reeling over this whole shoplifting thing, and I'm even more stunned that it's my grandmother who's delivering the news to me instead of Tyler. I rush over to the next building and pound on the door. After waiting a full minute I try again.

"Come on, Tyler. I know you're in there."

KNOCK! KNOCK! KNOCK!

"I'm not going anywhere until you open this door!" Finally I hear someone approaching the door and feel a surge of triumph. However, after the locks are disengaged and the door swings open, I'm the one who's surprised. "Mr. Jamison! I'm sorry, I didn't know you were home."

"I think that much is obvious." He runs his hand over his head. "Come on in. I think that Tyler is in her bedroom, trying to ignore me. You're more than welcome to see if you can get a little more out of her than I did, if you want." He steps back and allows me to pass through.

"Thanks." I enter the apartment and take one glance around. The place looks like a hurricane hit it.

"Excuse the place," Mr. Jamison says. "I've been busy and Tyler has been stubborn."

I flash him a half smile of understanding and then make my way through the living room and then down the hallway to Tyler's bedroom where I knock on the door.

"She's not going to answer," her father says. "She'll think it's me, and I think she has on her iPod."

"Oh." I glance at the door and then slowly turn the knob.

Surprisingly, it's not locked. "Tyler?" I push open the door and slip my head inside.

On the bed, Tyler is propped up on a mountain of pillows and bobbing her head. When she glances up and see me, there is some relief. A smile curves across her face.

"Hey, you," I say, easing into her private sanctuary. "Long time no see."

Tyler pulls the white ear plugs from her ears and sits up. "I'm surprised that he let you in."

"I came by after school, but no one was here or no one answered the door."

"Me and my old man are sort of engaged in a little game."

"Oh?"

"Yeah. We're trying to see who can stay mad the longest. I'm going to win this one hands down."

"Ooookay." I stretch my eyebrows and decide to let her just have that. I've never understood her and her father's games anyway. I step over piles of clothes on the floor and then find a clean spot on the bed and sit down. "So how are you doing?"

She shrugs. "All right—considering."

I nod and then fold my arms.

"I guess that means that you've heard," she says.

"Heard about what?" If she can play dumb then so can I.

Tyler glances away. "You know what."

I'm quiet for a moment because I'm both confused and disappointed in my best friend. But telling her that surely isn't going to help matters much, and lately it is way too easy to put my foot in my mouth and land on Tyler's bad side. It was just a month ago when I told her I understood why her mother left her. "Do you want to talk about it?"

She huffs. "What is there to say? I screwed up. I was at the wrong place at the wrong time—"

"Or you were hanging out with the wrong crowd?"

Another huff. "Michelle and Trisha are all right."

"How can you say that? Look what happened!"

"What? Like we've never shoplifted before?"

"Yeah, like when we were younger."

"Right. We're sooo old now." She makes a face and then rolls her eyes.

"We're old enough to know better," I tell her and then have to remind myself not to jump on her, but to offer support. "Anyway. I'm didn't come here to lecture."

"Well, that's a relief. I'm getting more than I care to count with Leon out there."

My eyebrows jump. Since when did she start calling her dad by his first name? "Are you all right? Are you not coming back to school or something?"

"I wish I didn't have to. The whole thing is a waste of time anyway."

"You don't mean that."

"Hell yeah, I mean it. I can't stand that damn school. I don't belong there."

"Are you serious? We've been planning to go to high school for, like, forever. We were supposed to all get popular, date the finest boys in school and to work our tails off to get into the best colleges."

"I don't recall that last part being on my list."

"Okay, college was my goal. But the rest of it we talked

about endlessly during sleepovers. The homecoming dances, the football games, now the basketball games and the proms. Don't you remember Kierra is supposed to make our dresses?"

A small smile hooks one corner of Tyler's mouth. "God help us. She will probably dress us in fluorescent pink or lime-green siesta dresses."

"Come on. It won't be that bad."

Tyler's eyes narrow on me. "When was the last time you saw me in a dress?"

"Fine. You can go in a pantsuit or a tuxedo for all I care, but you are going."

"Whatever." She rolls her eyes and waves me off.

"What, now you don't want to go?"

"It's a long way off."

"What are you talking about? The homecoming dance is in, like, two weeks."

Tyler rolls her eyes. "You want to go our freshman year?"

"We're supposed to go every year. Come on. We've talked about this."

"Well, I'm not going. So stop hounding me about it."

"What about basketball?" I ask.

"What about it?"

"You've made the team. Don't you want to play anymore?"

"Puh-lease. How long do you think they'll let me play once my grades come in?"

"I don't know. How about you do your homework and show up for class and see what happens?"

Tyler cocks her head. "You know, this is starting to sound like a lecture." She bounces off the side of the bed and stomps her way over to her nightstand. "I hate that school!" Tyler pulls open the top drawer and grabs a Baggie. Next she rushes over to her bedroom door and locks it.

"What are you doing?" I ask suspiciously.

"Nothing. I just want a smoke." She shrugs her shoulders and then makes her way back over to the bed. Once she's sitting beside me I see what's in the bag and my eyes nearly bug out of my head.

"Tyler! You smoke weed now?"

"Shhhh!" She bumps into one side of my shoulder. "What are you trying to do, get my old man to bust in on me or something?"

While my mouth is still hanging open, Tyler dips over the side and reaches under the bed where she proceeds to pull out an old Nike shoe box. Next thing I know I'm watching her gut out some type of cigar thingy, and then she reaches for her bag of weed. I'm just watching her and shaking my head. Who is this chick?

Tyler licks, rolls and then lights up. After taking a deep pull from her handmade blunt, she holds the smoke in her lungs and then passes the damn thing over to me.

I shake my head. "No, thanks."

"Come on," she squeaks while still holding her breath. "Don't knock it until you try it." She pushes the blunt toward me again.

"I *said* no." I move and then climb off the bed.

"Don't be a bitch and go out there and snitch to Leon."

Bitch? "How about you stop being an ass?"

"Uh-oh." Tyler exhales. "It looks like you're reconsidering giving me that lecture."

I open my mouth and then close it. What am I supposed to say? Something that I know she already knows? Still, I have to try something, right? "I'm just trying to understand what's going on with you. You're not acting like the Tyler I've known all my life. Hanging out with Billie Grant's crew? Shoplifting? Smoking pot?"

"You're lecturing," she warns.

"Well, maybe you need it," I snap. "What am I supposed to do, just watch you make one mistake after another? What kind of friend would that make me?"

"One that's a lot easier to be around."

"So now you want to crack jokes?" I fold my arms. "Nothing good has ever come from the road you're traveling down, and you know it. You want to be the next Billie Grant, is that it? The bitch is a loser who is never going anywhere and will likely be living right here ten years from now just like her mother and grandmother. Do you really want to peak at fourteen?"

"You're still lecturing," she says, drawing in another toke.

"And you're still being an ass!"

Tyler's brows pop up in amusement at me. "Are you finished now?"

"Look, and I say this with love, you're going to have to get your shit together. I understand that you're hurting."

Tyler's eyes cut away.

"You miss your mom. Hell, I miss mine, too. And I'm pretty sure that Kierra misses hers, as well. But at least you still have one parent, who, it's clear to everyone but you, is doing all he can to reach you."

"Yeah, I remember just how much he tried when he forgot I existed."

"That was then. This is now!"

"So I'm supposed to just forget about that."

"Yes! Forgive and forget. That's what you're supposed to do." I start to move toward the bed. "He was devastated when your mom left just like you were. And seeing how he is now, I think you're devastating him all over again because you're here, but it's like you've walked out on him, too."

Silence.

I shake my head. "I love you, Tyler. You're more than a best friend. You're like a sister to me. But I have to tell you. I'm disappointed in the choices you've been making lately. Get your head out of the clouds and start facing reality. Because the bottom line is that you hurt people, too, by shutting them out."

Finally she glances up at me with glassy eyes. "Are you through now?"

In one ear and out the other. "Yeah." I head toward her door. "I'll catch you later."

fifteen

Romeo—You're Not Listening

I'M making stupid mistakes on the football field. I can't seem to catch, throw or execute the simplest play because I can't get Anjenai off my mind. It started when I caught her talking to Kwan after gym class the other day, and then today I saw him walk her to her locker. What's going on with them? Are they a couple now?

I'm not going to lie and say that it doesn't bother me that she can move on so quickly. And who is this dude, anyway? Just because he can spit some rhymes and dress all right girls are losing their damn minds over him. I think Shadiq was right to be suspicious of him. I'm not down for just letting anybody into our private circle, but Chris tries to invite the dude to everything. I think Chris knows I don't like the homeboy, but he has Kwan tagging along as some kind of payback for that little fight in the locker room. And when he presses me on why I don't like the new guy, what am I supposed to say—that I don't like the way he's always hanging around my ex-girl?

Larry "T-bone" Owens charges and tackles me from my blind side. Next thing I know I have a mouthful of grass and the coach is blowing his whistle.

"What the hell was that, Blackwell?" Coach Irving shouts from the sideline. "Are you sleeping out there?"

"No, sir!"

"You can't prove that by me! You haven't completed a play yet!"

All eyes are on me. I suddenly feel like the headliner of a freak show. "I'll pull it together, coach!"

"You better!" He blows his whistle and we all huddle for the next play. *Concentrate. Concentrate.* But that's easier said than done. The whistle blows, the ball is passed and I try to spot my open man before throwing the ball. Larry charges and my mind goes blank again.

"Grrl."

I'm hit again. This time I land hard on my back and am left to try and blink yellow stars from my eyes. When my vision clears, Larry is there reaching a hand down to me to help me up. "Thanks, man."

Coach Irving is blowing his whistle like a toddler having a conniption fit. When he finally finishes, he orders, "Get off the field, Blackwell! Your playing today is jacking up my high blood pressure."

"Yes, coach!" Despite my disappointment, I run off the field with my head held high.

"Simmons, get in there! It's your turn to show me what they've been teaching you up in New York."

"Yes, coach!" Kwan grabs a helmet and runs out onto the field.

It takes everything I have not to stick out my foot and trip him up. I watch him as he huddles with his scrimmage team. Yes, I'm rooting for this guy to stink on the field. No point in trying to deny it. Being the star quarterback has always been my role, and I'm not liking it the least bit that this dude was able to just walk onto the team when we've already started our season.

The players line up in defensive formation. Coach Irving blows the whistle and Kwan drops back and I watch this boy throw a perfect spiraling ball down the center to Chris, who, in turn, takes off like a superhero toward the goal line.

"Now *that's* what I'm talking about!" Coach Irving shouts. "That's how we play some damn football."

I'm getting dizzy because my eyes are rolling to the back of my head so much. So what? The boy can throw. Big deal. By the end of practice, I'm so hot under the collar I don't know what to do.

"Good practice, man," Kwan says, running up to me and offering me his hand. Why the hell is he in my face lying? Everybody knows that I played like shit today.

"Yeah. Yeah. You, too."

Kwan frowns at me. "Yo, man. Did I do something to you that I don't know about?" he asks straight up.

This is my chance to tell this brother to back the hell up off Anjenai, and please believe that it's on the tip of my tongue when I see Phoenix suddenly popping up and waving as she rushes toward us. I groan. "Naw, man," I lie. "I'm just upset with my performance today."

A smile stretches back across Kwan's face. "Well, I know how that is. We all have our good and bad days."

"Yeah. Whatever."

"Hey, guys," Phoenix says, finally catching up to us. "Had a good practice?"

I roll my eyes.

"It was pretty good," Kwan answers for both of us. Two seconds later, my boys and the other Redbones join the circle. And everyone is talking about going to Club Zero, a teen nightspot that caters to the hip-hop and R&B crowd.

"Chris has been telling me that the club hosts a rap battle every Thursday night."

Bianca thrusts her breasts up on Kwan's arm. "Are you thinking about going up onstage?"

I lift a brow. I would love it if Kwan would take an interest in Bianca instead of Anjenai.

"Maybe. Right now I just want to check the place out, see who the real competition is in this town."

Chris is nodding his head. He's been to Club Zero hundreds of times, and he has yet to find the balls to take the mike. It doesn't stop him from criticizing all the performances and advising how he'd have done differently. Not that I doubt my man's commitment to music. I've listened to his flow for years. He's good. But there's something about getting up onstage and doing his thing in front of thousands of people that pulls him up short. Maybe Kwan will help him get over his stage fright.

"So are you down or what?" Shadiq asks, pulling me out of my silence.

I really don't want to hang with this dude. "I don't know. I've got a lot of homework I need to get caught up on."

Six pairs of eyes narrow on me like I've just sprouted another head.

"Maybe next time," I say.

"Hold on," Phoenix tells the group and then starts pulling me aside. "What's up with you?" she hisses.

"Is that a real question?"

"What? This means that you're going to mope for the rest of the school year?"

"Well, I certainly don't feel like dancing and celebrating. And you shouldn't, either." I pull her farther away from the crowd. "By the way, when are you going to quit the cheerleading squad?"

"Quit?"

I'm surprised that the thought hadn't occurred to her. "Phoenix," I say, trying not to laugh, "jumping, tumbling and falling can't be good for the baby."

"I'm fine. The baby's fine," she says defensively. "I'll quit before I start to show."

That doesn't sound right. "What does the doctor say?"

"Doctor?"

"You haven't gone to a doctor yet?"

"Why? I've got plenty of time."

That doesn't sound right, either. "Tomorrow we need to find a doctor. I'm fairly certain that you're supposed to start seeing them long before you just start showing."

"How do you know? Did you suddenly grow a uterus or something?"

"What?"

"How about you just leave the prenatal care stuff to someone who knows a little more about the female body than you do, okay?"

"What? I can't go to the doctor's appointments with you?"

She rolls her eyes as if my questions are bothering her. "Why do you need to go? Are you going to be the one on the table trying to push something the size of a bowling ball out of you?"

I wince and even clutch my stomach at the very thought. "No."

"Then why do you need to go?"

"I don't know. I thought I at least needed to be there to coach you through the delivery."

"That's Lamaze classes, and that's a totally different thing."

"It is?"

"See? You don't know anything. Like I said, leave all the prenatal stuff to me."

I'm already tired of arguing. "All right. Fine."

"Good. So let's go to Club Zero with our friends tonight." She slides up against my sweaty chest. "Who knows? Maybe afterwards we can crash at my place. My parents left to visit my aunt in Florida this morning. They'll be gone until Sunday night."

I frown.

"Come on," she purrs. "It's been a little while since…you know." She gives me a look that I definitely recognize.

I don't believe this. I shake my head. "Phoenix—"

"Don't start trying to play all hard to get. I'm still fine, and I know that despite what we've been through this year, you still want to get with this."

I try not to laugh but it's damn hard. Instead, I step back and continue to shake my head. "That's not going to happen."

The smile falls from her face. "What? You don't find me attractive anymore?"

"No. That's not it."

"Then what? You can't be scared that you'll knock me up. I'm already pregnant, remember?"

I drop my head into the palm of my hand and try to massage my growing headache away. "I'm talking, but you're not listening," I tell her. "We're going to have a baby together, but *we're* not going to stay together. We can put on a front for everybody while you're pregnant. I don't want anyone to think that I'm just abandoning you."

"But you *are* trying to abandon me."

"I'm supporting you through the pregnancy. That's it. After that we can work out details on how to raise the baby either between ourselves or with lawyers. I don't care which. But we are *not* getting back together—in any shape, way or form. Got it?" With that, I turn away and head toward the gym for a hot shower. The whole while I can feel Phoenix's gaze blazing a hole in the back of my head, and frankly, I just don't give a damn.

sixteen

Phoenix—The Twilight Zone

DON't *panic. Don't panic.* I pull in several deep breaths as I watch Romeo storm back toward the gym. But it's sort of hard not to panic. The whole plan is to get Romeo to get me pregnant again without him ever knowing that I lost the first pregnancy. Now he's making it perfectly clear that he has no intention of ever sleeping with me again.

So what am I going to do now? I have no idea.

"So are we going tonight or what?" Bianca asks, stepping up behind me.

I slam my eyes closed in order to give myself a quick second to pull myself together. "Yeah. Why not? We can go without him," I say, turning and putting on a bright smile.

My girls give me a look that questions my ability to control my man. Hell, I'm starting to question it myself. *He'll come around.* I've been telling myself that a lot lately, because in the past it has always been true. But it doesn't feel true anymore. In fact, I'm still fighting this feeling of doom and finality that's moving in between Romeo and me. And I can't help thinking that this entire thing still has something to do with Anjenai.

I don't get it. What can Romeo possibly see in that scrawny freshman, anyway? Isn't she, like, a nerd or something?

"Are you all right?" Raven asks, coming to my other side and swinging an arm around my waist in some lame attempt to act like she really cares.

"Yeah, girl. He's just tripping because he thinks I should be stepping down off the cheerleading team. You know Romeo, he's just so concerned about the baby."

"Ah," they say, nodding their heads. Lying that Romeo is concerned about my health and the baby's is a hell of a lot better than letting them know that he simply doesn't give a damn about me anymore.

"Actually, I was wondering the same thing," Bianca squeaks. "It can't be healthy for you to be tumbling off pyramids and stuff."

"Puh-lease. You just want to be head cheerleader," I tell her.

She glances toward Raven and shrugs. "So?"

My brows jump. Is this heifer actually going to be bold enough to admit it to my face? *My, my, my. The worm is turning.*

"What's the big deal?" Bianca asks. "If you can't be head cheerleader, then why can't one of us try out for the slot? Or can the spotlight only fall on you?"

Both she and Raven raise their brows at me, and I feel ganged up on. "I never said that."

"You didn't have to," Bianca says. "You act like it. In fact, you always just expect us to play second and third fiddle like it's your due or something."

"I do not."

"Yes, you do," Raven says, frowning and crossing her arms. "We've been nothing but loyal and supportive toward you since grade school. You, on the other hand, act like you're just tolerating us. And you're always suspicious. Like we're always trying to get what you got."

"Well, aren't you?" I challenge. Time out for all this two-against-one BS. "You think I don't know that you gossip behind my back? The only reason that you two sniff up after me is that you secretly want to *be* me."

"WHAT?" they thunder in unison.

"Oookay," Chris says. "I think that this is where we exit stage left." He looks to Kwan and Shadiq. "Come on. Let's hit the showers while they have this catfight. Something tells me it's not going to be pretty." He and Shadiq snicker, but Kwan casts us a sympathetic look.

My brows knit together while I wonder what that's all about. As he heads back toward the gym behind Chris and Shadiq, I finally take a good look at him. Bianca and Raven didn't lie in describing him. He is definitely fine, and rumor has it that he is just as good on the football field as Romeo.

Bianca steps into my line of vision. "No. You're not checking out *my* man."

I roll my eyes at them. "He's *not* your man—yet. And no, I wasn't checking him out, I was just—"

"Bitch, I just saw you," Bianca squeaks at the top of her voice. "You got some nerve, you know that?"

"And you're delusional, too," Raven chimes in. "We want to *be* you? Where the hell you get that nonsense? We ain't a couple of ugly chicks. And we got our own shine. Our parents are rolling just as fat as yours. So what do I want—blond hair? I can buy that shit in a bottle. You might have a little more ass, but your tits are MIA. All right? Bianca and I have been nothing but loyal to you, and we get nothing in return."

"That's not true."

"No? Then how come you never told us you were pregnant? How come we had to find out along with the rest of the school? We're supposed to be your best friends. We have never kept a secret from you. And all this mistrust and secrets—how the hell do you think that makes us feel?"

I fold my arms. "Okay. Now you're just being overly dramatic."

"No. We're being real. Did you even notice that we had your back at Shadiq's party when Anjenai and your own sister jumped you? Do you even care? Or at this point do you just expect it?"

"I…" A lump of emotion clogs my throat.

"You know what?" Bianca says. "Forget it. Maybe it's just time that we all do our own thing. That way you don't have to be constantly glancing over your shoulder looking for whatever shine you think you have."

The Redbones break up? "What, I'm supposed to kiss your ass now?"

"See. You're clueless," Raven says. "You do you and

we're going to do us, okay?" She grabs Bianca by the arm and then tugs her toward the gym.

I'm stuck standing there looking like Boo Boo the Fool. First Romeo walks out on me, and now my girls. What the hell?

seventeen

Nicole—Why Weight?

seven *pounds!* I can't believe it. I'm down seven pounds in a week! I step off the scale and dance around in my bra and panties like I'm one of Beyoncé's booty-shaking backup dancers. If I can keep it going for seven more weeks, then I can hit my goal weight right before Christmas. Ooh. Wouldn't that be a nice Christmas gift to myself, being able to slide into a pair of jeans in a single-digit size. Man, if I'm skinny by Christmas that still gives me plenty of time to find a boyfriend before the prom.

"Wheeeeeee!"

Thump!

I quickly quiet down. The last thing I want to do is wake up my mom. The rare times that she's up in the morning, she's a pain in the ass. As fast and as quietly as I can, I wash my face and put on the few makeup items I own—some foundation, mascara, and lip gloss. After that, I pull the black scrunchie out of my hair and run the brush through my brown curls. Now, I know seven pounds isn't much when one weighs nearly two hundred pounds, but I swear that I can almost see a difference.

"Christmas," I whisper to myself. I can't help imagining strolling through school in a pair of tight, skinny jeans and winking at all the cute boys and then pretending to be hard to get. *I can't wait. I can't wait. I can't wait.*

I exit the hall bathroom at the same time that my mother's bedroom door swings open. But instead of Cruella De Vil waltzing out, it's my father. We both freeze and stare at each other in shock.

Then, slowly, he starts working his mouth, but no words come out. This is an unusual situation for us. Sure, I know my parents hook up from time to time, but I have never known him to actually spend a whole night here. Does this mean that there is trouble in his marriage and once again he's turned to the arms of his favorite mistress?

"Humph! Good morning, Nikki."

I hate it when he calls me Nikki. "Morning," I say, folding my arms.

"You're, uh, up early."

How does he know what time I get up? "Not really."

"Honey, you almost forgot your watch." My mother slithers up beside him.

I can't help turning up my nose at this satin-and-lace number that she's wearing. It leaves very little to the imagination.

"Um, thanks, honey." He smiles sheepishly and then tilts his head in my direction so she could see that they had company.

My mom's eyes slide lazily in my direction. "Oh, Nicole. You're up."

This really is a bad performance. "I'm up because I have to take the bus to school," I tell them and then take a jab. "Unlike my sister, who gets to drive. Maybe I should ask her to start picking me up in the mornings. You know, I think it's time that we start hanging out more." I roll my eyes and then march down to the kitchen.

There, I grab a coffee cup, fill it with water and then heat it up in the microwave for a full minute. Since dear old Dad didn't immediately race out of the house I just assume he's giving my mother grief for letting him get caught with his hands in the cookie jar, so to speak. Why not? He likes blaming other people for his mistakes. I don't see why this should be any different.

The microwave beeps and I remove my hot water and grab my lemon and cayenne pepper. This crap tastes horrible, but as long as it's doing the job then I'm going to stick with it. I take my first sip of this disgusting concoction and twist my face up at it. At the same time, I hear my father's heavy footsteps make their way toward the kitchen. I back toward the microwave and grab the bottle of aspirins sitting in the basket on top of it.

"Nikki," he starts, sounding way too jubilant.

I hope his ass doesn't think I'm about to cook him some breakfast or something. This isn't the Happy Hooker Inn, where you get a complimentary breakfast after cheating on your wife.

"I was just talking to your mother, um, a few minutes ago about your situation."

What situation? I just look at him.

"Well, I think you raised a good point about Phoenix having a car and you being forced to take the school bus every day."

Okay. Now he has my undivided attention.

"So what do you say that this weekend I take you out to a dealer friend of mine and see about getting you your own set of wheels? You think that you'd like that?"

"Really?" I ask, unable to stop the smile and volcanic emotions erupting inside of me. "This weekend?"

His own smile stretches across his face, causing his blue eyes to start twinkling. "You got it, sweetheart."

I set my hot water down and rush to throw my arms around him. This is something I haven't done since I've been old enough to comprehend that I'm just his bastard child and not his golden princess, Phoenix.

"Uh, I guess that means that you like the idea," he says, awkwardly.

I blush and step back. "Yeah. It would really be great!"

"Good. It's settled." He coughs and clears his throat. "I guess I'll see you this weekend."

I bob my head and can't wait for him to leave so I can jump up and down. He's halfway to the door when he stops and pretends like he just remembered something.

"There's just one thing," he says, snapping his fingers.

"What's that?" I ask.

"Um, what happened here this morning," he starts. "You know, between your mother and me. I can trust you to just keep that between the three of us, right? I mean there's no need for Phoenix or her mother to find out that

I, um, occasionally spend time with you and your mother, right?"

Since when has he spent time with me? "Right," I assure him. "It's just between us."

His smile returns, and he even adds a wink. "Great. I knew I could count on you. I'll pick you up this weekend." He turns and rushes out of the house.

The minute the door slams behind him, the smile slides off my face. I've just been bribed. I try to decide how I feel about that. Maybe it'll depend on the type of car I actually get. If it's a small economy car, pretty shitty. If it's a Range Rover, pretty good.

"Impressive," my mother says from behind me.

I don't even have to turn around to know that she's smiling like the Cheshire cat.

"I'm starting to think that you have a little of me in you after all."

Oh, God, I hope not.

BFF Rule #10

Never bad-mouth a friend to others.

eighteen

Kierra—Burning the Candle at Both Ends

I've dodged a bullet. I'm not pregnant. From the moment I read the results on that pregnancy test until now, I really feel like I've been given a second chance to straighten up and fly right, like Anjenai's granny likes to say. I feel so good about my situation that the few times I've passed Chris in the hallway or in the lunchroom, I can't help smiling at his childish butt. My sudden shift in mood causes him to stretch his brows curiously at me. But for the most part I just dust my collar off and keep it moving.

As for my promises to the man upstairs, I've been studying, cleaning the apartment and cheering my ass off on the field. The first two weeks were a breeze, but this current week is sort of kicking my butt. There's only so many hours in the day, and it seems as if I'm getting less and less sleep or, rather, it seems like the moment I lay my head down it's time to get up.

"Oh, my God! This is your whip?" I exclaim when Nicole pops up Monday morning at Oak Hill. Anjenai,

Tyler and I are standing in front of our apartments with our mouths literally hanging open.

Nicole beams as she steps out of her fresh, red Range Rover. "Isn't it beautiful?" she gushes. "My father bought it for me this weekend."

"Obviously," I gasp, running my hands over its sleek lines. "Looks like things are getting better between you two, huh?"

Nicole cocks her head. "Please. This is a bribe."

"A bribe?" the three of us ask in unison.

"Yeah. I caught him spending the night with my mom last week, so he doesn't want his delusional wife and Princess Barbie to know that he's still on the creep over at our house."

"Wow," Anjenai says. "That's pretty deep."

"Not really." Nicole shrugs. "My dad loves keeping secrets and manipulating people. I basically just added my name to the list."

"Don't feel so bad," Tyler pipes up. "He probably could have bought me over with a ten-speed bike."

We laugh.

"Well, c'mon and hop into your new morning ride," she declares. "If I'm riding in style, then so are my best friends."

Please believe that she didn't have to say that twice. We all reach for the nearest door and pile inside. I take a good whiff of that new-car smell and melt into the leather interior. "I'm officially jealous."

"Make that two of us," Anjenai says from behind me. "I want to pinch myself, and it's not my car."

"Yeah, well. We'd better roll up out of here before some-one decides to jack us. This isn't the suburbs, you know."

I roll my eyes. "Puh-lease. Who on earth gets jacked at seven in the morning? You know all those boosters ain't up this early in the morning."

Tyler bobs her head. "True that."

Nicole starts the vehicle, and it's so damn smooth that I can hardly tell that the damn thing is even on. We roll out and can't resist throwing up our middle fingers at the group of losers standing in front of the property waiting for the school bus.

"SO LONG, LOSERS!" we shout and then start laughing at everyone's stunned expressions. During the ride to school, we turn the radio to V-103 and start bumping along with their jamming morning show.

"Damn. I know I could get used to this," I say.

"I hear that," Tyler co-signs.

"Well, you're going to get used to it, because this is going to be y'all's ride from now on."

"Except on the days we have practice after school," I tell her.

"I don't know. Maybe we can work something out," she says.

"For real? I can't believe my ears."

Nicole shrugs. "That's what best friends do for each other, right?"

We all smile back at her. I don't know about my girls, but I certainly appreciate her offer. I'm running around so much lately that shaving off waiting-for-a-bus time will help tremendously.

"Well, you don't have to worry about me. I'm dropping off the basketball team," Tyler announces.

"WHAT?" Nicole and I thunder. "WHY?"

Tyler shrugs. "It's just not my thing."

"Are you kidding?" Nicole says. "You're great. You and Anjenai both. You guys are naturals and Jackson High's key for the freshman team to make it to the championships."

Tyler shakes her head, and I recognize from the look on her face that nothing we're going to say can change her mind.

My gaze swings over to Anjenai and she looks like she's positively seething. I want to ask if there is something going on with them again, but decide against it. Whatever it is, I'm sure I'm going to find out eventually.

When we pull into the school's parking lot, all heads turn. No lie. We all feel like major rock stars when we open the doors and stroll up to the school. Everybody is going to be buzzing about us, and it won't have anything to do with jumping on any damn body. That'll be a nice change.

"Ayo, Tyler!"

We all turn our heads to see Michelle Todd and her Siamese twin, Trisha, waving Tyler over.

"I'll catch up with y'all later," Tyler tells us and then takes off.

I frown. "Is it just me, or did we just get dissed for Billie Grant's old crew?"

Anjenai shakes her head. "It's not just you." She looks at me. "Did you know that Tyler got nabbed for shoplifting a couple of weeks ago?"

"WHAT?" Nicole and I yell.

Everyone in the hallway swivels their heads in our direction, and then I ask in a lower voice, "Are you kidding me?"

"Does it look like I'm kidding?" She glances off in the direction Tyler went. "She and her two new pals skipped class and went over to that strip mall and got busted."

"So what happened?" Nicole whispers.

"She has a court date coming up. I don't see how she won't get juvie time."

"For shoplifting?" I ask. "I thought you got something like community service or something for a first-time offense?"

Anjenai and Nicole stare at me.

"What? I had a cousin get busted. You remember my cousin Melanie?"

Anjenai nods. "Yeah, but this wasn't just a couple of items. From what Granny told me it sounds like they were straight looting the place."

I'm completely stunned. *What's going on with that girl?*

"Morning, Anje."

I glance up to see Kwan tossing my girl Anjenai a flirtatious wink before keeping it moving. The three of us watch as he struts by, my gaze checking out the cute tush on him. "Sooo, what's with that?" I ask her.

"Hmm? What?"

Nicole and I share a look.

"Now I know you ain't going to stand here and say that you didn't know that fine brother is giving you the I-want-you eye?"

"What? Nothing."

I stare her down.

"Really," she insists.

"I can't tell if you're lying to me or to yourself. Either one I find disturbing."

Nicole chimes in. "All I know is, if you want him, you better make a move before Bianca scoops him up." She nods her head down the hall and we both look to see Bianca trying to glue herself to the boy's hip with all that giggling and cheesing that she's doing.

"Now, *that's* embarrassing," I say. "Why don't she just hand him her panties and call it a day?"

"Hoes don't wear panties," Nicole snips.

We look at each other and burst out laughing.

For the next week, I get a kick out of, as well as I believe most kids in this school, watching Romeo watch Anjenai. It's so clear to anyone with eyes that he's not over Anjenai. That day at my locker, I thought he was just giving me lip service, but I don't think that anymore. Still, despite the big puppy-dog eyes, I don't know if I can bring myself to root for him. Anjenai seems to be moving on, and I'm happy to see it.

Tyler is another story entirely. I don't think she knows what's going on with herself. When Anjenai told me about the shoplifting, I was surprised, but, after thinking about it for a while, not so surprised. I mean, I love Tyler, but she seems to be all over the place. And now with her court date coming up, I agree with Anjenai—I don't see how she's going to get out serving a little time in juvie. She picked the wrong store and the wrong mall for that nonsense.

Unlike Anjenai, I've elected not to say anything to her

about it. The last thing I'm in the mood for is Tyler picking a fight with me about something that *she* did. Life is too short for that BS. I'm just going to support her and hope that eventually she'll come around.

Nicole is styling and profiling since her father bought her Range Rover despite the fact that she just has a learner's permit. Plus, I think she's losing weight. Her jeans are loose and she's looking pretty good.

"Ms. Combs, very good," Mrs. Ruckers, my art teacher, exclaims from over my shoulder.

I'm pulled out of my reverie to glance down at my abstract drawing. "Thank you."

She leans closer. "You're really talented, Kierra. Have you thought about a career in art?"

I perk up and tell her proudly, "Actually, I want to be a fashion designer."

"Oh. I would love to see some of your designs."

"Really?" I'm stunned. No one has ever taken an interest in my drawings other than Anjenai and Tyler, and I have to say that it's quite an ego boost.

"Sure, bring them into class tomorrow," she says, smiling. "You might also want to consider doing a piece for the art festival this spring. I think that you'd do well."

Inside I'm lighting up like a Christmas tree. "I'll look into it."

Mrs. Ruckers winks and then moves on to the next student. I sort of faze out and start daydreaming about entering the art festival. Of course that means I'll have to create something, and just when am I going to find time to do that? I'm already burning the candle at both ends.

I'll figure something out.

Hopefully.

nineteen

Anjenai—Say Yes

I think I like Kwan, despite my vow to stay away from boys for a little while. I'm also pretty sure that he likes me, too, because every time I turn around he's right there smiling and trying to talk to me. This fact never ceases to amaze me because I don't doubt that he could have any girl he wants. Bianca comes to mind. The girl is pulling out all the stops, but I can't gauge how he feels about her. The last thing I want to do is to get caught up in another love triangle. One time is more than enough for me.

Still, some of the same insecurities I felt with Romeo are starting to crop back up. Things like Kwan and I being from two different worlds. His of privilege and mine not so much. I'd tried to merge those worlds before, and I ended up with egg on my face.

But still I wonder.

"So how long are you going to have me just make googly eyes at you?" Kwan says, strolling up to me after I've changed for basketball practice.

"What?" I ask, turning.

"Don't play all innocent on me." The side of his face kicks up a smile. "You know exactly what I'm talking about." He stretches an arm over my head so that he can cage me in between him and the wall.

I lift my brows and try to level him with a serious look, but instead I end up smiling because of the way his warm breath tickles the side of my neck. "What are you doing Thursday night?" he asks.

"Why you want to know?"

The other side of his face balloons into a smile, causing his two dimples to wink at me. "Because a brother might be trying to ask you out."

My heart is doing all kinds of flutters and backflips, but at the same time I'm trying to keep my head from floating into the clouds. When something seems too good to be true, then it usually is. "I don't know if that's such a good idea," I say.

"What? You got a boyfriend or something?"

I'm blushing so bad that my face is at least ten degrees hotter. "I didn't say that."

"It's a direct question, li'l ma. You got a man?"

Whoo, Jesus. I'm going to pass out. "No."

Kwan leans down closer. "Then how come you won't go out with me?"

"Maybe I don't like you. Have you ever thought about that?" I ask, folding my arms because I need an extra protective barrier between us.

"Actually, that thought has occurred to me several times,"

he says. "If it's true then I'm determined to change your mind about that."

"Really?"

"Yeah. And I want to start by taking you out to Club Zero."

"A club?" I shake my head. "There's no way I can pass for twenty-one."

"Nah. Nah. It's this teen club out in Alpharetta. Some friends of mine on the football team took me there a couple of weeks back. It's really cool, and they have these rap battles that I want to get in on."

"Oh. You think you're ready for the big stage."

"A brother like me stays ready." He inches even closer. "You never know when an opportunity might present itself. You know what I mean?"

Be still, my heart. "Has anybody ever told you that you're pretty cocky?"

Kwan laughs. Its husky sound is also doing a number on me, and I'm afraid what little will I do have is quickly dissolving. "I think you're confusing that with *confidence*."

"Is that right," I whisper and then try to swallow the growing lump in the center of my throat.

"That's right." His gaze falls from my eyes to watch my tongue dart across my lips. "Say you'll go out with me," he says.

I'm tempted.

"You know that you want to."

I do want to. But am I ready to put my heart back out on the line so soon?

"Come on," he whispers. "I promise I'll be on my best behavior."

That wins another smile from me. "All right," I finally say. "One date. What time do you want to meet there?"

"No. No. No." He takes my hand and surprises me by brushing a soft kiss against the back of it. "We're going to do this right. I'm going to pick you up at your place, introduce myself to your parents and then drive us to the club and bring you back home. You know, like a real date."

Suddenly the idea of him coming to the projects and then introducing him to my grandmother and four bad-ass brothers is enough to make me start reconsidering this.

"And you can't back out now," he warns. "You already said yes."

I bite my tongue and when he hands over his cell phone I enter my address and phone number into his address book. *I really hope I know what I'm doing.*

twenty

Kwan—You Remind Me

I ain't going to lie. I've been sweating Anjenai from the moment I saw her. No, she's not laced in the tightest gear, blinged out or weave-o-rific. She's pretty, though she doesn't try to boast it, and just one look in her eyes and you can tell she's smart as hell. And when she's working the court, she completely blows everybody else away. I love an athletic woman, and Anjenai has all the makings of a star.

Plus, she reminds me of my ex-girlfriend, Charmaine, back in New York. Charmaine was killed by another teenager from our school who was texting and driving. It was a head-on collision that the coroner said had killed her instantly. When I first got the news it was the first time I'd cried since I was, like, a toddler. It really hurt losing her, especially since she'd just left my place after we'd had an argument. I know we used to argue all the time, and the fights now seem so silly in hindsight. But they usually started with Charmaine accusing me of checking at some girl that I wasn't and getting her cobra-neck on.

I've had the same problem with the few girlfriends that I've had in my life: insecurity. They either became overly jealous or too possessive. Both traits would lead me to eventually ending things like I had the day Charmaine was killed. I hate to admit it, but I was a bit relieved when my parents told me that we were moving to Atlanta. It meant that I would be spared returning to my old school where all my well-meaning friends and teachers would talk to me and treat me like a fragile piece of glass.

But then I come here and run smack into a girl who looks a lot like Charmaine. Well, if her hair wasn't in braids and she maybe wore more makeup. The first time I laid eyes on Anjenai I thought I was seeing a ghost. When I realized that she wasn't, I started noting that despite their similar looks, Anjenai and Charmaine were definitely two different people.

Anjenai intrigues me more. I can tell that hanging with her will be more meaningful than just hanging out at malls and constantly trying to outshine the teenage Joneses. Anjenai holds the potential to be a triple threat: homie, lover and friend. At least that's what I'm going to find out.

At football practice, this dude Romeo is still giving me serious face. I wish that he would just spit out what's on his mind so we can squash whatever nonsense he thinks we're beefing over, because all these side glances are working my last nerve.

"Yo," I say, walking over to Chris. "What's really up with your boy?"

Chris glances out onto the field toward Romeo. "Man, I done told you not to pay him no mind. He got female trouble. NawhatImean?" He elbows me and then tosses down a cup of Gatorade.

"Yeah. I've been doing that, but the situation seems to be getting worse," I tell him. "Me and the dude don't have to be friends or nothing, but I'm getting tired of him mean-mugging me every time I turn around. Either you need to talk to him or I'ma have to step to him and handle it. *NawhatImean?*"

"I hear you." He smirks and then cuts his gaze toward me. "Are you still peeping out that freshman?"

"Who—Anjenai?"

"That will be the one."

"Yeah, so?"

"So that was the girl he was trying to holler at about a month back."

I shrug. "And? You said that he stepped off."

"I didn't say that it was his choice. His future baby mama ran interference and I suspect he regrets the play."

The pieces of the puzzle have now clicked into place. I glance back out to the field to see our star player throw a thirty-yard pass. *Good arm.* Once it is completed, Romeo removes his helmet and casts another look in my direction. "Well," I say, turning my attention back to Chris, "I say his loss is my gain."

twenty-one

Anjenai—Make Me Over

"I'm so jealous!" Nicole screams, grasping hold of her steering wheel as we cruise down the back streets toward the Oak Hill Apartments. "How is it that you keep getting all the cute guys?"

"That's what I want to know." Kierra laughs. "First Romeo and now Kwan? You need to be doing an advice column in the school newspaper or something."

"Okay. Now y'all are just blowing my head up instead of telling me what the hell am I going to wear to go to a club? Not to mention he wants to come over and meet my family."

Kierra cracks up. "I can just see it now. The twins making kissy noises at y'all and Hosea and Edafe bugging him to hold his wallet."

I can't help smirking. "Ain't that the truth?"

"And don't forget, your granny is going to want to know *all* about his peoples. Where they come from, which church they go to—and now she'll probably ask whether he's knocked up some hoochie mama before he landed on her doorstep."

"Arrrgh. Why did I say yes?"

Kierra leans forward between the two front seats. "Because according to your grades, you're not dumb. Can you imagine what it will do to Romeo when he finds out that you're dating Kwan?"

Rolling my eyes and shaking my head I ask, "Why the hell should he care? He's made his choice."

Nicole cuts a look over at me.

"What?"

"All right. Real talk? We all know that Romeo is not over you. That boy roams around that school like a lost puppy. Frankly, I think my sister overplayed her hand. There's even word floating around that the Redbones broke up."

"You're kidding," Kierra and I shout, flabbergasted.

"I know. Stop the presses, right? From what I understand there was some blowup and Phoenix accused Raven and Bianca of wanting to be her."

"What's the problem? That's true, isn't it?" I ask.

Nicole shrugs. "Who knows? All I know is they haven't been talking since."

I sit back and let that marinate for a minute.

"I think you need your own column, too," Kierra says. "How is it that you get the scoop on everything?"

"People talk when they think I'm not listening. And despite popular opinion, boys gossip waaay more than girls. Believe me."

"Well, none of it matters. I could care less whether Romeo misses me or not. I. Don't. Miss. Him."

We all fall silent.

"I mean it," I say. "I could never forgive him for what he did to me that night. The humiliation. The—"

"We know," Kierra and Nicole say. "We were there."

"Then you understand where I'm coming from," I nearly yell. "It's over. I'm done. I hope he and his baby mama have a long life together. Me? I'm moving on. And why not Kwan? He's nice, talented and charming. And he's willing to meet my family. Romeo never did much more than drop me off after practice or grab a slice of pizza."

"Sounds like someone has already made up her mind," Kierra says.

I nod, realizing that I had. "It's just one date."

"Hmm. Humph."

We all giggle.

"I still don't have anything to wear," I remind them, and then reach up and flip down the visor. "And I need to do something to my hair."

"Oooooh," Kierra and Nicole coo and share another knowing glance. "It's like that."

"What? It's the first time I'm going to a club—teen or not. What if they have something like a velvet rope and the people at the door take one look at my wash-and-wear outfit and laugh me straight out of the line?"

"That would be embarrassing," Kierra agrees.

"Yeah. It'll be like Shadiq's party all over again," I say. "Anjenai Legend is up at the club trying to stunt in cotton and polyester." I shake my head. "I ain't trying to go out like that."

"So what do you want to do?" Nicole asks. "You want to

have, like, a pajama party and we give each other a make-over or something?"

Kierra perks up. "Yeah. We can, like, take your braids down and straighten your hair, and I can teach you how to put on makeup."

Nicole gasps. "Let's do it! When is your date again?"

"Thursday."

"Then let's do it Wednesday night. You guys can spend the night at my place."

"Oh. I can't," Kierra whines. "I have to watch my sister in the evenings. Can you spend the night at my place?" she asks Nicole.

"In Oak Hill?"

I roll my eyes. "Girl, ain't nobody going to bother you."

"What about my car?"

"Well, that's another story." I laugh. "You're going to have to work something out on a ride. You can't park something like this at Oak Hill and expect it to still be sitting there when we wake up the next morning."

We have a good laugh about it, but we hammer out our plans for a pajama party. Later that evening, I swing by Tyler's to invite her over, as well. But when she opens her apartment door, I'm stunned to see that she's already got her party going.

"Heeey," she says after cracking open the door. A goofy smile slops across her face, and her eyelids are drooping low. Inside, music is bumping and I can hear people laughing and giggling.

This girl is high. "Oh, I'm sorry. I didn't think you had

company," I say, noting that she doesn't bother to invite me inside. I stand there and pretend that I'm not hurt.

"That's all right, girl. What's up?"

"I, uh—" I glance over her shoulder and catch Michelle sitting on some dude's lap and attempting to swallow his tongue.

Tyler cocks her head and I swear I can hear her thinking, *Why don't you take a picture? It'll last longer.*

"Kierra, Nicole and I are going to have a, um, sleepover at Kierra's Wednesday night, and I just came over to invite you, too." Suddenly talking to Tyler about sleepovers seems so childish. Her new friends are older, and clearly they are into other things. So surely playing with hair and makeup won't be high on Tyler's list of fascinating things to do.

"Wednesday, huh?"

"Yeah."

She shakes her head. "I don't know. I have court Wednesday…so I guess it'll just depend on whether the judge gives me my freedom papers or I have to head off to juvie for a little while."

How did I forget about her court date? "Oh. I'm sorry. I forgot. Um. Yeah. Well, I guess we can just talk about it in the morning when Nicole picks us up. I'll let you get back to your friends." I turn to leave.

"Actually," she says, stopping me. "I'm probably going to be riding with Michelle and Trisha tomorrow."

I didn't know that they had a car. "Okay…then lunch?"

"Actually—"

"You know what? Just whenever—or forget it. I don't

want to come between you and your *new* friends." I turn to storm off again.

"C'mon, Anje. Don't be a bitch."

"Stop calling me that," I snap. "Because if anyone is being a bitch lately it's *you!* I don't even recognize you anymore."

"Is this going to be another lecture?" Tyler asks, looking bored.

"Damn, Ty," Michelle says, coming up for air. "You gonna hang out in the hallway all night or what?"

"I gotta go," Tyler says. "We can continue this later." Without another word, Tyler draws back her head and then closes the door in my face.

twenty-two

Tyler —Purple Haze

ANJE and her lectures. I'm really not in the mood.

"Who was that at the door?" Kerosene asks, looking up from the sofa. It is so weird having him here without his girlfriend, Adele, attached to his side. But rumor has it that they are beefing these days, and he, instead of his girl, continues to hang thick and heavy with our clique. I guess it don't matter. He's good people.

I just ignore him and float my way back over to my spot in Leon's armchair.

"Well?" Kerosene repeats, toking another hit from his fat blunt.

"Why you want to know? It wasn't for you."

Michelle detaches her lips from her new man's lips long enough to throw in a chuckle. I don't know if I like her new boo. He's kind of old—like nineteen. Why someone out of high school still wants to mess around with a fifteen-year-old is beyond me. But by the time the blunt that's in rotation makes its way to me, I put that foolishness with my list of others—in the back of my mind.

"Are you nervous about your first court date?" Trisha asks, handing me a beer from the six-pack they brought over with them.

"Naw," I lie. "This shit is what it is, right?" I shrug my shoulders. "I mean what's the worst they can do—send me to juvie? That's no biggie."

Trisha's lips spread into a fat smile. "Pretty much. Hell, at this point that place is like home away from home. Ain't that right, Michelle?"

We both glance over to Michelle and her *old man* on the couch only to see them going at it. Moaning and groaning and old boy has his hands up the front of her shirt and rubbing on her tits like he's trying to make a wish or something.

"I swear she's such a ho," Trisha says.

I laugh and shake my head. My buzz is setting in real good now.

Kerosene reaches over to the table and grabs the last beer. "Trisha, we out of beer."

"And?" she snaps.

"And go get some, girl!"

"Me?" Trisha swivels her head around. "Fool, have you lost your mind? What the hell is wrong with your legs?"

"I brought this pack. It's your turn to start chipping in," he snaps. "You always at a party but you don't ever want to chip in. What the hell is that all about?" He gives her a hard glare.

Finally she rolls her eyes and spits, "Fine! I'll go get the beer." She turns toward me. "Tyler, you want to come with me?"

"No," Kerosene interrupts. "She's going to stay here and keep me company." He looks over at me. "Ain't that right, Ty?"

I just shrug because I really don't feel like walking or even leaving these people in my apartment while I'm gone. One time Stella brought her thieving butt over here and I had to put her ass in check.

Trisha rolls her eyes at us as she pushes herself up off the floor and then stumbles her way toward the door. "I'll be right back."

"Whatever." Kerosene smirks. "Bring back some chips while you're at. I got the munchies, ma."

"Boy, I ain't no damn 7-Eleven." She jerks open the door and storms out.

I'm left sitting in my chair snickering at them.

"I swear that girl be working my nerves," Kerosene complains.

"She's all right." I close my eyes and try to float on top of my high.

"Hey, Tyler. Why don't you come over here and sit right next to me?" He pats the empty space next to him.

"Because I'm comfortable right where I'm at."

He chuckles. "Ah. You must be scared, then."

My eyes creep open. "Boy, you ain't nobody."

He continues to pat the sofa. "Prove it," he challenges.

I study him, especially that goofy smile and his twinkling eyes.

"Don't make me start clucking at you like a chicken," he says.

"Fine. Whatever." I push myself up out of my chair, stomp over next to him and plop down. "There."

"See? Now, was that so damn hard?" he asks, passing me the blunt again.

I wave it off. "I'm fine."

Kerosene's eyes rake over me as he licks his fat lips. "You sure are."

The brazen compliment takes me off guard, and I can't come back hard with a snappy reply. Instead, my face heats up in embarrassment.

He spreads his arm out behind me. "Can I ask you a question?"

"You just did," I tell him.

"Nah. I mean, like, a personal question," he says, moving in so close I'm now aware of his body cologne.

I flutter my gaze away from his. "What is it?"

He edges closer. "How come you ain't got a man?"

Oh, God. I'm blushing.

"Hmm?" He reaches for my hand and starts playing with my fingers. "I mean, you're a good-looking chick. A little buck wild with that temper, but I just think you ain't met the right man to reel you in line."

"Reel me in?" I cut my gaze up at him. "Boy, you done bumped your head."

"Nah. Nah. I've been checking you out for a minute. Matter of fact, you're the reason me and Adele have been beefing."

"Me?"

"How come you think I always want to come hang over here? I'm feeling you, girl."

"Yeah, right."

Closer. "I'm being serious." He brushes my hair from my shoulder. "You're the type a brother like me could get down with. You know. A ride-or-die chick."

Our eyes lock together, and there is this fusion of energy that seems to suck all the oxygen out of the room because I'm suddenly dizzy as hell.

"I got another question," he says.

"Wh-what is it?" I whisper.

"Mind if I kiss you?"

Now my heart feels like a jackhammer pounding against my chest. He wants to kiss me? For the first time, I look at him outside of being just a friend. I guess he's pretty cute with his shoulder-length dreads and his pencil-thin goatee. *What is he—sixteen—seventeen?*

I'm quiet for so long, I guess he takes my silence as a yes and starts to lean in the remaining few inches that separate our mouths. When his lips touch down onto my lips, I'm shocked at the feel of his warm tongue snaking into my mouth. Then I slowly start to melt. He tastes wicked, like some forbidden fruit. So why don't I stop him when his other arm wraps around me and then pulls me close?

Because I like it.

"All right now, you two." Michelle giggles. "Y'all know I'm going to tell."

Kerosene pulls back, and I immediately miss his mouth.

"Let's go back to your room," he whispers.

I'm nodding before I even process what he said. Next thing I know, I'm taking him by the hand and leading him to my room. It's the first time in my life that I'm a little embarrassed about the place looking like a pigsty. "Excuse the mess," I say.

"Don't worry. It ain't no thing." He sits down on the edge of the bed while still holding my hand.

Now what am I supposed to do?

He cocks a smile up at me. "Now, don't get all shy on me," he says, dropping my hand and then pulling off his T-shirt.

Nice chest. I gulp this huge knot that's been building in my throat. *Should I tell him that I've never done this before?* I weigh that question for a couple of seconds and decide that if I share that information he just might run out of here screaming and I don't want him to leave. Finally, I decide to follow his lead and pull my shirt off, too.

That puts a big old smile on his face. He reaches for me again, and the next thing I know I'm being pulled down onto the bed and planted under him. That's fine because all that matters is that I get to have another taste of his mouth.

Warm.

Hard.

Powerful.

"Are you on the pill, baby?" he rasps.

"The what?" Hell, I can barely think and he's asking me questions.

"You know, birth control."

"Oh. I, um, no. I—"

"No matter. I got something." He reaches in his back pocket and produces a condom.

My heart goes at it again. But when he starts kissing me again, all my anxieties disappear along with my clothes. So lost am I in all the things that I'm feeling and tasting that when the pain comes I'm completely caught off guard. I start punching at his chest.

"Whoa. Whoa. Whoa, l'il ma." Kerosene grabs both my hands and pins them down on either side. "It's just going to hurt for a few seconds." He starts to move again. "See?"

The pain does go away.

He smiles down at me. "I didn't know I was going to be your first." He leans down and kisses me again. "That makes me feel kind of special."

We go back to kissing and other things. I'm so lost in the clouds he's creating inside my head that I don't hear the ruckus that's going on outside my bedroom. But that all ends when my father bursts into my bedroom like a roaring lion.

"WHAT IN THE HELL?"

"DADDY!"

twenty-three

Nicole—Baby Phat

TWelve *pounds!* I'm giddy and jumping around in the bathroom again. I'm well on my way now. I can see the small change in the mirror, and yesterday Kierra asked if I was losing weight. All I have to do now is stick with the program. Sure, I tend to get a little light-headed sometimes in the middle of the day, but it's a small price to pay for such great results.

I quickly get dressed, rush down for my hot lemon water and cayenne pepper breakfast and then jot down a note to remind my mom that I'm spending the night at Kierra's before rushing out the door to pick up my best friends. I'm all bubbly and happy, but it's clear that something's up when Anjenai and Kierra pile into my ride.

"All right. Who died?" I ask, hoping to lighten the mood.

Anjenai huffs. "Nobody. Let's just go."

That's clearly a lie. "Shouldn't we wait for Tyler?"

"She has court today," Kierra reminds me.

"Oh, yeah. I forgot. Maybe I should go over and wish her luck?"

"You're more than welcome to try. That's if she doesn't slam the door in your face."

"Ooookay. What's going on? Y'all fighting again?" I ask.

"Apparently. Only I didn't get the memo," Anje says. "Can we please go?"

I glance back at Kierra, who only gives me a shrug. "All righty, then." I shift into Reverse and hope the girls just fill me in on the way to school. But halfway through the drive, it's clear that I'm going to have to do my own interrogation if I'm going to get to the bottom of things.

"Sooo, what happened?"

Anjenai, who's staring out the side window, starts shaking her head, but then a lone tear slips down her face and she quickly swipes it away. "I don't know anymore." She sniffs. "She's not letting me in. She's…she's acting like someone I don't even know."

"It's that Michelle and Trisha," Kierra accuses. "We should have seen this coming."

"And done what?" Anje snaps, still sniffing and wiping up her tears. "It's not like we can tell her who she can and can't hang out with. That girl has a hard head and it's just getting harder. And—" she glances down at her hand "—you know what? Let's just forget about it. Sooner or later, she's going to snap out of this and come to her senses. I know it."

I feel at a disadvantage since I haven't been friends with the BFFs that long. I don't know how Tyler was before they came to Jackson High, but I do know in the short time that

I have been around them, Tyler tended to be a little all over the map. She's tough, but cool, and a lot of times seems to be her own worst enemy. I like Tyler. I told her as much on the first day of school when I heard that she had broken the female school bully's nose. But it doesn't take a rocket scientist to figure out that she's dealing with a lot of stuff she doesn't like to talk about.

I can relate.

"Don't worry," I try to console Anjenai. "She *will* come around. There's not a whole lot of true friends out there."

Anjenai nods her head. "Yeah. Maybe."

We're quiet for the rest of the drive to school. It kind of makes me wonder what the mood is going to be later tonight during our sleepover. After we park and climb out of my ride and head toward the school, Anje stops and looks me up and down.

"Are you losing weight?"

I beam. "Yeah. Just a little bit." I don't want to brag too much because I a) don't want to jinx it and b) want to stun them when I finally stroll in here with my fabulous new body.

"Looking good," she says. "Keep it up."

I just smile and stroll on into school. After stopping off at my locker, I swing into one of the upstairs bathrooms. While I'm in one of the stalls, I can't help hearing someone crying a few stalls over. *Oookay.*

I quickly do what I have to do and rush to wash my hands so I can get out of there. But when I turn to go I spot the pale pink Chandra Bulgari purse Phoenix got for Christmas on the stall floor.

"Phoenix?"

The crying stops.

"Phoenix, is that you?" I walk over to the stall and then knock on the door.

"Nicole?" Phoenix croaks.

"Yeah. Open up."

"Is there anybody out there with you?"

"No. I'm by myself."

"Lock the bathroom door."

I turn and rush to the main door and turn the silver lock. "Okay. It's locked. Now come out." She stands and shuffles stuff around before unlocking the stall and creeping out. Quite honestly, I'm astonished to see that she's not on point like she usually is. Her hair could use a brush through it a couple of more times, and I'm not sure she put her makeup on when the lights were on. Given how much I've always hated Phoenix, I'm surprised to feel sympathy and compassion for her right now.

"I look that bad?" She turns toward the large mirror above the sinks. "Oh, shit."

"Are you sick or something?" I ask, moving from the door. "Do you have morning sickness or something?"

She laughs. "No. I wish I did." She goes to the sink and starts washing her makeup off. But while she scoops water onto her face, she suddenly starts crying again.

What the hell? I approach the sink and awkwardly try to pat her on the shoulder. "There. There. Everything is going to be all right."

"No it isn't," she sobs. "Romeo hates me. Raven and Bianca hate me. *You* hate me."

I flinch. "Now...I..."

Phoenix sniffs and raises her head to meet my gaze through the mirror. "Don't lie. You hate me."

Instead of lying, I don't say anything.

Just as quickly, Phoenix's gaze falls away. "I don't blame you. It's not like I've ever treated you like a real sister."

You got that right. I remove my hand from her back and then fold my arms underneath my breasts.

She frowns and looks me over. "Are you losing weight?"

And just like that she is officially on my good side. "Here, let me help you," I say, propping my purse up on the counter and digging out my makeup bag. It isn't her usual Make Up Forever or MAC, but in a case of emergency Cover Girl will have to do. First I take a couple of paper towels and blot her face dry, and then I get to work.

The school bell rings for homeroom, but I stay put until I at least make her look more presentable. For her part, Phoenix stands still while I put a little more color into her face. It's odd. Me doing something nice for her, and her being humble.

"I really appreciate you doing this for me," Phoenix says.

I stop and stare at her.

"What?"

"That couldn't have been easy to say."

She opens her mouth, but I quickly cut her off.

"And don't *you* lie to *me*."

She laughs and, in that moment, there's a thin bond threading in between us. One that I would have never dreamed could exist just this morning when I woke up.

I'm actually dreading when we finally have to walk out of here.

"You're probably wondering why I'm looking like such a wreck," Phoenix says.

"Running through a list of things in my head right now."

She drops her gaze again while her lips twitch for the right words, but they don't seem like they're coming any time soon. "Look. I understand. You don't have to tell me. I just wanted to help. If I could."

When our gazes lock again, her eyes start filling up with tears.

"Please don't ruin my work. We'll have to start all over."

Her smile returns, but just for a brief moment. "If I tell you something, could you keep it a secret?"

Great. Another family secret.

"I mean it. *No one.*"

This sounds serious. "All right. I won't tell anyone."

She stares at me as if she's having second thoughts, and then she drops a bomb on me.

"I lost my baby."

twenty-four

Romeo—Competition

I can't stand Kwan. I can't stand the way he talks. The way he walks and how he's always hanging around my boys, smiling and cheesing like he belongs in my crew. He doesn't. And if he doesn't get up out of my face pretty soon, we're going to have to knuckle up.

"Romeo!" Shadiq snaps and then waves his hand in front of my face. "Damn, man. Don't you hear me talking to you?"

"What?" I pull my gaze from Kwan and Chris talking across the cafeteria.

Shadiq laughs. "Man, you need to chill out with that nonsense."

Confused as to what we're talking about, I glance over at him.

"Kwan," he says. "You keep mean-mugging him like that and he's gonna take it personal."

"Puh-lease. I wish he would step sideways to me."

"What's your beef, man? When I told you I didn't like

him you spat this whole peace-and-brotherly-love bullshit at me, and now you clocking him like a full-time job." He leans over. "This wouldn't happen to have something to do with Anjenai, would it?"

"What?"

Shadiq shrugs. "Chris seems to think that you still have the hots for the girl."

"Don't be retarded." I roll my eyes, but my acting skills are failing me.

"I don't believe this. You already have the hottest chick in this place knocked up and now you can't let go of some chick you chilled with for what—a couple of weeks?"

I don't answer. There's no way I will be able to get him to see where I'm coming from. I was truly feeling Anjenai. I miss talking to her, playing ball and hanging out at the Mellow Mushroom and hogging down pizza. *Damn. How did I screw this up?*

"Whatever, man. I wasn't born yesterday."

I pick at my crappy Hamburger Helper lunch and, like a thousand times before, try to figure out a way to reboot things with Anjenai. So far I haven't come up with a single plan.

"Whatever. We can squash it. You coming out to Club Zero tomorrow night?" Shadiq asks.

I groan. "I don't know, man. I got a lot of shit I got to do."

"I think I'm going to go up onstage," he says, smirking.

This surprises me. "For real?"

Shadiq shrugs. "Kwan says he's going up, and I can't have him trying to outshine the kid, you know?"

"Ah, so you still don't like him, either?" I smirk. "And here you are sweating me?"

"I ain't wishing death on the brother or nothing, but I'll be damned if I'm just going to let him move here and step into the spotlight I've been creating for years. You feel me? I've been grinding and handing out mixtapes since sixth grade. People been waiting for me to break for a minute. This dude rolls down here and tries to show me up at my hangout joint? It's not going to happen."

"All right. All right. I feel ya," I tell him. "Yeah, I'll roll through and show you some love. Not a problem."

"Cool. Cool." He bobs his head and casts a glance across the cafeteria at Kwan. There's gotta be some kind of irony about both of us feeling threatened by the same dude.

Shadiq and a few teammates from the football team make their way over to our table about the same time Phoenix strolls in. The minute she's in my line of vision my head starts hurting and my lunch sours in my stomach. But I have to push all that stuff aside and try to dust off my acting skills again.

"You mind if I sit here?" she asks, fluttering a weak smile at me.

I shrug. It's hard to mask that I don't really care where she sits. I do need to go a little easier on her. I know that she and her girls Raven and Bianca are still beefing. Too much negativity probably isn't good for the baby.

Phoenix sits down, still smiling.

"I didn't know you were here today. You weren't in homeroom this morning. Is everything okay?"

"Yeah. Everything is fine."

How come every time I talk to her lately, the hairs on the back of my neck stand at attention? I study her. "Have you been to the doctor yet?"

"Here we go," she says, rolling her eyes. "I thought we already agreed to leave all the prenatal stuff to me?"

That's starting to annoy me. "What? Now I can't ask anything about the baby? Is that it?"

"How about you ask about me? You ever thought about that?"

"Oookay," Shadiq says, jumping up from his seat. "I gotta run and do something." He waves me off. "I'll catch up with you a little later."

On cue the other brothers on the team stand and follow, leaving me to deal with Phoenix on my own. When I look back over at her, she cuts her gaze away.

"What's going on with you?"

"What do you think?" She works her neck a bit and then folds her arms. "I've never been in this position, and here you are stressing me out and treating me like something that stuck to the bottom of your shoe. I feel like I'm all alone in this." Her eyes start filling up with tears. "It's not fair. And to be honest, I never thought that *you* could be so cruel."

"Me?"

"Look at what you've done to me. I'm turning into a joke in this school, all because I had the audacity to get pregnant. You want to walk away and go play house with your next bitch."

I plant my elbows on the table and release a deep sigh. "Phoenix, we've been over this—"

"Yes. And we're going to keep going over this until you come to your senses. Yeah, maybe I was a bitch and a tease before, but now things have changed—I've changed. I'm going to have your baby now. And I think we at least owe it to our kid to try and work things out. If it doesn't work out down the line—fine."

Her pleading eyes are getting to me, and I find myself longing for something strong to drink instead of this damn carton of milk.

Phoenix reaches for my hand. "Romeo. We've been together a long time. You can't sit there and tell me that it's always been bad. You used to be crazy about me. You're the reason I got kicked out of private school, because you used to sneak into my dorm room. We have history. We had plans. Whatever you do, don't abandon me now."

As I stare into Phoenix's hazel eyes, old emotions start tugging on my heart. We have had some rather fun and wild times together. And there was a time when I thought that one day she'd be my wife, after college and a few years in the NFL. But things changed—my feelings changed when we started high school, a full year before Anjenai came onto the scene. Suddenly we were fighting more, and she was always pulling one outrageous stunt after another. They were all designed to get a rise out of me, and they all succeeded.

"I don't know, Phoenix."

She squeezes my hand. "Don't you? I'm telling you that I've changed. Carrying this baby has changed me. And I know more than ever that I want us to bring this child up in the world together. You loved me once. I know that you can love me again and *our* child."

From the corner of my eye, I see Anjenai and her posse stroll into the cafeteria and stop in front of Kwan. She's all smiles and looking happy. *She's moved on.* Admitting that to myself is like suffering a death.

"Okay," I whisper, returning my attention to Phoenix. "We'll give it another try."

Phoenix lights up and pops out of her seat. Before I know it, she's throwing her arms around my neck and smothering me with kisses. "You won't regret this. I promise!"

I hope she's right. I pull back with a smile and glance back toward Anjenai, only for our gazes to lock…but only for a brief moment.

twenty-five

Tyler—My Day in Court

LEON and I are not talking.

After he embarrassed me last night trying to kill Kerosene, I pretty much decided to shut down all communication. I absolutely refuse to talk to him, so much so that I slam my bedroom door in his face. Then, two minutes later, I hear a drill. Next thing I know he's completely taken my door off by its hinges and he's shouting that I no longer have privacy privileges.

Asshole.

I didn't even want him driving me to court, but it's not like I really had a choice in the matter. During the entire drive he's trying to coax me into talking to him. When that doesn't work, he starts swearing and hitting the steering wheel. It doesn't matter what he says, I will never forgive him for what he did last night. *Never.*

As far as walking into the courtroom, my nerves don't really hit me until I have to go through the security check when you first walk through the door. The tall, bulky officers, waving metal detecting wands and searching through my personal items, irk me a bit. I don't like this sense of helplessness that comes over me.

Leon inquires where we need to go, and we follow a lady officer's directions to a tall wooden door at the end of a long corridor. I chug in a few deep breaths, but feel my knees start to buckle as I get closer to the door.

I can't do this. I can't do this.

I want to pause and wait a minute, but Leon is right behind me, and he pulls the door open and reveals this huge wood-paneled courtroom. That's when I feel the first wave of tears burn my eyes.

"Come on," Leon says, pushing me forward. "No point in getting all scared now."

I hate him. Walking into the courtroom I stroll down the aisle, thrusting up my chin and feeling like I've just been cast in an episode of *Law & Order.* We're told by one of the clerks to just take a seat in one of the pews. I see Michelle and Trisha in the front row and start to head in that direction when my father grasps me by the elbow and steers me in the opposite direction.

"I don't think so, little girl," he says grimly.

That's his problem. He still thinks of me as a little girl. Now with my butt planted firmly on a dark wooden pew, I sit ramrod straight, arms folded and doing my best to ignore Leon. I hope he can feel just how much I hate him right now.

"I can't believe I'm missing time at work for this crap," he swears under his breath.

Work, work, work, work. That's all he cares about.

I feel his eyes shift toward me. I know that he wants to say something—probably the same lecture he gave me in the car, this morning in the kitchen and yesterday in my bedroom after he chased all my friends out of the apartment. I mean, really. How is he going to bitch about me smoking weed when he still tosses back alcohol when he thinks I'm not looking. Everybody knows that alcohol is far more worse than marijuana.

"You know, I'm halfway hoping that the judge does give you a little time in juvie. Maybe that's the only way you'd see just how good you have it."

Good? Maybe I should ask whether he's high. I turn in my seat and see the pews are filling up pretty fast. Will all these people hear about what I got caught doing? They just discuss everybody's business out in the open like this? My stomach starts twisting into knots.

"Psst, Tyler," someone hisses from behind me.

I jerk around and then perk up in surprise to see Kerosene two rows back, waving and winking at me.

"What the hell is *he* doing here?" Leon demands with his face twisted in rage.

I smile and break my code of silence. "Maybe he's here to lend support. I doubt that you know much about that."

Leon refocuses his glare on me, but I just smile smugly in his face.

The clerk stands as the bailiff moves to a corner of the court and instructs, "Everyone rise to your feet for the honorable Judge Daphne O'Connor."

I stand and watch the porcelain-white female with fiery-red hair piled into a bun on top of her head stroll into the courtroom draped in a black robe.

More knots twist in my gut. I don't have a good feeling about this.

"Please have a seat." The judge's stern voice slices through the silence.

My knees fold without me thinking much about it, and for the next hour I'm left to stew in my nervousness and fear. When my case is called, Leon has to tug on my sleeve to draw my attention. I take one look over my shoulder and receive a thumbs-up signal from Kerosene and, remarkably, I feel just a tiny bit better at least until I make my way up to the defendants' table. The charges are rattled off, and I feel as if I'm standing in the center of a bright spotlight.

"Shoplifting, huh?" Judge O'Connor repeats, I guess for the people in the back row.

My court-appointed attorney enters my plea and then proceeds to inform the judge about how this is my first offense and blah, blah, blah. It turns out that the facts that I'm not some model student or have much of a do-good community service track record mean that I don't receive much leniency.

"All right, Ms. Jamison, I've heard enough. After reading both the report of the mall's security guard and the police report and taking into consideration the amount of goods that was stolen from the department store, I'm sentencing you to serve six months in juvenile hall."

Six months!

After she bangs the gavel and then two officers start toward me.

What? Right now? I glance over to Leon only to see him hang his head. "Aren't you going to do something?"

"I'm sorry, baby. I'm going to check and see when visiting hours are."

Visiting hours? One of the officers directs me to turn around, and the next second I feel the cold, hard steel of handcuffs being locked around my small wrists. Again, my gaze floats toward the back of the courtroom and I see Kerosene, pushing his chin up and reminding me to be strong. I smile, and in return he kisses two fingers and then holds them up as I'm being pulled to the side door.

"It's going to be all right, baby," Leon says; his voice trembles with emotion. Even then, I can't help feeling anger and resentment. I really do think our relationship is broken for good.

I remain silent as the cops pull me across the threshold and then close the door. Juvenile hall, here I come.

twenty-six

Kierra—A New Friend?

I'm bone tired. Between school, cheerleading and my responsibilities at home, I truly feel like that candle I'm burning at both ends is dangerously close to meeting in the center. I think I'd be able to sleep better if I knew where Deborah was. I haven't seen her since the evening she dropped McKenya and me off in front of the Rite Aid. Usually she's in bed asleep when we get up in the morning and just leaving for work when I get home from cheerleading practice. But her bed is empty in the mornings, and McKenya is sitting home alone when I get in from school to start dinner. I asked McKenya once where Deborah was, and she just shrugged her shoulders and kept on watching her cartoons.

What the hell?

I've really been trying not to panic, but that's not working anymore. I'm starting to think that she pulled the same stunt as Tyler's mom. I can't tell if she packed anything because she has so much shit, I can't tell if something is missing or not. Yesterday, I called the Champagne Room, but trying to get information out of management about one of their dancers was impossible. Maybe she's been getting in after we leave for school and leaving earlier for some reason or another. Calls to her cell phone go straight to voice mail, and pleas for her to call home go unanswered.

So many times I have picked up the phone with the intention of calling the police to report a possible missing person, but each time I had to hang up when I thought about Child and Family Services showing up at the door and marching us to two separate foster homes. We have to stick together.

But food is running low at the house, and I'm going to have to figure out some way to get some money. I hope I won't have to get a job or something. Where on earth will I find the time to squeeze in a job?

Because of my lack of sleep last night, I conk right out in the middle of algebra class. Just when my trip to la-la land starts getting good, I feel a nudge at the back of my chair.

"Go away," I groan. For some reason I think it's McKenya waking me up because she wants some breakfast. The nudge becomes a kick at the back of my chair.

"Ms. COMBS!"

My head jerks up from the desk at the sound of Mr. Griffin's raspy baritone. "Yes, sir! What?"

Everyone snickers because I've just been busted. My face burns with embarrassment while my gaze drifts toward Chris. His smirking face makes my blood boil.

Mr. Griffin, a Morgan Freeman look-alike, is clearly annoyed as he crosses his arms and stares down over the tops of his glasses. "I was asking you the answer to the problem on the board that you're supposed to be working out."

"Oh." I rub the side of my face to make sure that I wasn't slobbering on myself. "I, uh—"

He shakes his head and I feel thoroughly chastised. "Mr. Hunter!" He pivots around and focuses his laser-like stare on Chris. "What about you? Surely, you've been working diligently on the correct answer?"

Chris becomes as ash-faced as I feel while nervously licking his thick lips. "Nah, nah. I got stuck working it out."

Mr. Griffin sucks in a deep breath. "Let me remind you kids. The key to solving every problem is just following steps. You don't have to understand it. You just follow the steps." He turns and moves down the aisle, finally calling on Miss Know-it-all, Allison Hart, who's having a conniption fit waving her hand at the back of the room, for the answer.

Minutes later, the class bell rings and I struggle to drag myself out of my chair. Just a couple more classes and then I can catch some Zs while Nicole drives us back to Oak Hill. Of course then I'll have to cook dinner and then find the strength to host a pajama/makeover party. I roll my eyes. I wonder if it will be considered rude if I fall asleep in the middle of my own party.

"Ms. Combs?" Mr. Griffin calls out to me before I'm able to escape his classroom.

Drawing a deep breath, I slowly turn around and face him. "Yes?"

He plops behind his desk and waves me over.

My shoulders drop. I'm really not in the mood for a

lecture. I thread through a stream of kids going in the opposite direction until I reach Mr. Griffin's desk in the corner of the room.

"Is everything okay with you?" he asks, getting straight to the point.

"Yeah," I lie effortlessly. Unfortunately, he doesn't look like he's buying it.

"Is there a problem with you not getting enough sleep at home?"

This time I just shake my head.

Mr. Griffin cocks his head and stares me down. "Since you don't seem to have much to say on the matter, maybe I should just discuss this with your parents?"

"Humph! Good luck with that. You'll need a Ouija board to talk to my father, and you'll need to be put on the visitor's list at the prison to speak to my mother."

The smug expression slides off his face. "Grandparents?"

"Never met them." I cross my arms.

"Who is your guardian?"

I pause.

Mr. Griffin shrugs. "I can just get the information from your school records."

This is the last thing that I need. "Look, Mr. Griffin. I'm sorry about falling asleep in class. I just stayed up too late last night talking on the phone. I swear that it won't happen again." I level him with my best puppy-dog eyes. It's not like I'm doing badly in this class, and I don't make a habit of falling asleep. I'm sure this is what's going through his mind while he studies me, because he finally starts nodding. "All right, then." He waves a finger directly in my face. "I'm going to be watching you, Ms. Combs. No more sleeping in my class."

"Yes, Mr. Griffin."

"All right. Off to your next class."

I quickly hightail it out of there before he changes his mind and decides to insist on meeting with Deborah—wherever the hell she is.

"Mr. Griffin giving you a hard time?" The voice floats out to me from my right, and I turn in time to see a skinny boy who looks as if he should be in junior high and not high school.

"Excuse me?"

He rocks his head toward the classroom. "The teach. He wouldn't have to worry about people falling asleep in his class if he'd at least make the damn thing a little more interesting."

I bob my head in agreement. "I didn't know you were in my class."

"Most people don't notice me," he says with a casual shrug. "That's the price I pay for being so short. Kierra, right?"

"Yeah...and you are ?" I ask as we start strolling down the hallway.

"Drake. Drake Brown," he answers with a head nod, and I smile. "I think I know what you need."

I frown. "What do you mean?"

"To stay awake," he says. "I used to fall asleep in class all the time. Between school, the school newspaper, the chess team, the track team—"

"You're on the track team?"

"I'm may be small, but I fly like the wind." He turns up a smile. "Not to mention, I have piano lessons, karate lessons and I do work with the VolunTeen program at the children's hospital."

"Wow."

"Volunteer work looks good on college admissions," he says. "I'm planning to go to Harvard."

"Impressive."

"What about you?"

"I don't know. Probably something like the Art Institute. I want to be a fashion designer."

"Better start researching that stuff now—and aim to get into the best schools for that sort of thing." He shrugs. "Maybe I can even help."

Is he hitting on me? "Yeah…maybe."

Clearly my answer disappoints him because his smile evaporates from his face.

"Well. I didn't mean to bother you or nothing. I just thought I could help you out with your problem. I guess I'll just see you around the way."

"Whoa. What's up?" I'm confused by the sudden change. I don't know the dude, but I'm both intrigued and suspicious about how he wants to help me. "So what did you do to keep awake in class?"

He glances around, and I do the same thing—not sure who we're looking out for. The next thing I know he's sliding something into my hand. When I start to look to see what it is, he hisses, "Hey, wait 'til you get to somewhere private before you peek at that."

Drugs.

"And don't worry. Consider that on the house."

"That's all right." I shake my head and attempt to hand it back to him.

Drake tosses up his hands. "Nope. It's a gift."

"I don't do drugs," I hiss at him.

"Girl, please, that stuff is harmless. Just think of it like a heavy dose of caffeine."

"Really?"

"It's just a little pick-me-up. Help you get through the day."

He looks honest, but I'm from the projects. It's the innocent-looking ones that you have to look out for. "All right. Whatever," I say, fully intending to flush his *caffeine* pills down the toilet the first chance I get.

But once I start to nod through seventh period, I pop those babies down my throat. And they definitely wake me the hell up.

twenty-seven

Anjenai—Girls' Night

SOME party. Nicole looks depressed, and Kierra…well, I don't know what the hell is up with her. We left Nicole's Range Rover in the student parking lot and rode the school bus back to Oak Hill, where we were mercilessly teased about returning to LOSERSVILLE. We laughed. Kierra talked a mile a minute about…well, I'm not quite sure about that, either, since it seemed to have a little of everything and followed no logical train of thought—at least not to me. Then again, it's been a little difficult to concentrate with my thoughts tangled up with excitement about tomorrow night and worry about how things went down with Tyler today at court.

Last night when Tyler slammed that door in my face, my only thought was: *To hell with her.* However, after a night of crying my eyes out, I realized that I didn't really mean it. I'm still hurt, but I love my friend and I just have to let her go through whatever it is she's going through. I never told Kierra and Nicole about Tyler's new weed habit. It didn't seem like my place, and it would feel too much like gossiping about someone we all cared about.

When we get to Kierra's place, I'm not surprised to see McKenya plopped in her usual position with her eyes on the television set. No doubt Deborah is just passed out asleep, since she works at night.

"Hello," Nicole coos in her friendliest voice to McKenya.

McKenya doesn't even bother looking in her direction.

I grin and tell Nicole, "Don't worry. It's not you." We take our overnight bags to Kierra's room, where teddy bears and fashion collages reign supreme. One thing about my girl Kierra is that she's incredibly clean and organized. Everything has its own special place, and she tends to go overboard to make sure things stay that way.

"Hold on for a minute. I'll be right back," Kierra says, leaving us alone in her room while she goes down the hall. I hear her knock on her sister's door, but a few seconds later she returns with a long face and her eyes glossed with tears.

"What's wrong?" I ask, rushing over to her.

Kierra looks up at me, blinks and then shakes her head with a smile. "Oh, it's nothing, Deborah just headed out to work early. I wanted to catch up with her and ask her something. That's all. Don't worry about it."

That's odd. "She left McKenya here by herself?"

Kierra shrugs that off, as well. "It's no big deal." Her smile stretches a little wider as she reaches for one of my braids. "I'm going to start dinner for McKenya, and then we're going to have to get started taking those braids down. That's going to take at least a couple of hours." She turns.

"Oh, well. I want to run next door to check on Tyler," I tell her. "I'm dying to know how her court date went."

"Yeah. Me, too," Nicole jumps in. "Since it's her first offense, I'm hoping that she just got a good smack on the wrist. Who knows, maybe now she realizes that she needs to leave those future jailbirds, Michelle and Trisha, alone?"

"I wouldn't count on it," I mumble, remembering last night again.

Kierra shrugs. "All right. Sounds good. Let me just tell McKenya we will be right back."

We all walk back through the living room. McKenya takes her sister's announcement with the same bored disinterest. Since Kierra and Tyler live in the same building, we aren't too concerned about leaving the apartment. However, the minute we start knocking on Tyler's door, that same anxiousness overcomes me. I'm not as optimistic as Nicole about Tyler just getting a smack on the wrist. And then Mr. Jamison answers the door with bloodshot eyes and rumpled clothes.

"Hello, Mr. Jamison," I greet him, glancing over at Kierra and Nicole. "Is Tyler home?"

"Um." He scratches the side of his face and then leans against the door frame. "I'm sorry, girls, but, um, Tyler is at juvenile hall." He scratches again. "She's gonna be there for a little while."

"How little?" I ask in a robotic voice.

"Six months," he says.

Six months? We all just stare at him.

"But I'll let her know that you came by to check on her," he says, filling the awkward silence and reaching for the door. "I'll see y'all around." He quickly closes the door, and we still stand there, a bit shell-shocked.

Kierra draws in a deep breath. "So much for that slap on the wrist."

"Yeah. No kidding," Nicole mumbles.

I'm fighting tears. I may be angry with Tyler, but I still love and care for her. We return to Kierra's apartment like a group of zombies. We sit down at the dining-room table, still darting glances at one another. It's clear we each want to say something, but what is there to say?

"Kierra, I'm hungry," McKenya whines after muting the television. "When are you going to fix dinner?"

"Right now," Kierra says, climbing back out of her chair.

"Here. Let me help," I say. I need to busy myself with something or I'll just pull my hair out. "So what are we cooking?" I open the refrigerator and blink in surprise. It's damn near empty.

"Wow," Nicole says behind me. "Looks like it's time to go to the grocery store."

"Uh, yeah. I've been meaning to go," Kierra says, wiggling in between us and closing the refrigerator door and then opening the freezer.

At least there is more food in there.

"We're having lasagna," she informs us and then grabs a big red box before heading toward the oven. "I figure that will be less work, and we can go ahead and get a jump on those braids."

I shake my head. "To tell you the truth, I don't feel much like going now."

"Why?" Kierra asks, ripping open the box.

"Because of Tyler's situation," I admit.

"Sooo what? You're going to make Kwan wait to go out with you for six months? That doesn't make much sense."

"I have to agree," Nicole co-signs.

"C'mon. We kinda knew this might happen. I don't like it any better than you, but if there's one thing I know for sure it's that Tyler can take care of herself. The girl is tough as nails."

She does have a point.

"Besides, I'll never forgive you if you let someone like Kwan get scooped up by someone like Bianca. She's already on him like white on rice and you need to show Romeo that you don't have any problem replacing his ass."

I laugh at that. "He could care less. Did you see him and Phoenix tongue boxing in the cafeteria today? They should've just gotten a room."

Kierra shoves our dinner into the preheated oven. "Actually, I was a little surprised by that. The last couple of weeks it looked like those two were breaking up. Didn't you think so, Nicole?"

Nicole is unusually silent during the gossip, so we both turn toward her. She's biting her lower lip as if it's helping her keep quiet.

"Nicole?"

"Um?"

Her innocent act needs a little more work. "What are you *not* saying?"

"Nothing," she squeaks.

Kierra and I fold our arms and stare her down.

"I...can't," she admits, frowning. "I gave my word to someone."

"Oh—your word?" I look at Kierra. "That sounds serious."

"It is. You have no idea," she says, but it's clear that she wants to spill the beans.

I stare at her harder, but when I know that she's just seconds from breaking, I decide to cut her a break and toss up my hands. "Well, that's very admirable. I don't want you to break your word."

"I don't know about that," Kierra says. "It depends on how juicy this information is."

"Veeerrrry juicy," Nicole says.

"Well, now you *have* to tell," Kierra says. "How can you just tease us like that? That's not right!"

I agree. "Who exactly did you give your word to?"

Nicole bit her lower lip.

"Phoenix?" I guess.

When she doesn't answer, I'm incredulous. "Since when are you and your sister tight enough to be exchanging secrets?" I'm a little put off by this latest development. Here we invited Nicole into our close circle, but if she's now building a bond with her bitch of a sister...well, it's a problem. Nicole clearly reads my expression and out the gate she starts tripping over her words.

"Look. I *know* what you guys are thinking. It's nothing like that. I just stumbled in on Phoenix, crying her eyes out—"

"Crying?" Kierra and I thunder. Probably because we have a hard time imagining Phoenix crying about anything.

Nicole holds up her hands. "Look. I've already said too much. She'd kill me if she found out that I told you guys that—" Nicole stops herself by slapping a hand over her mouth.

Kierra and I grab her by opposite arms and drag her back to the bedroom where we dump her onto the bed and then stand over her with our arms crossed.

"Spit it out," we demand.

"I can't," she whines, wringing her hands. "I promised."

Okay. This is going to require a different tactic. I sit down next to her on the bed. "Look, Nicole." I wrap my arm around her. "I think it's admirable that you want to keep your promise to someone. But to Phoenix? Think back to all the humiliation that she and the Redbones have put you through over the years. I mean, now that they've fallen out, she wants to turn to you for what? Sisterly love?"

"Yeah. That's mighty convenient, don't you think?" Kierra joins in. "Think about it. What has Phoenix *ever* done to deserve your loyalty? Where with us, you know we'll *always* have your back."

Nicole's gaze darts back and forth between us before she finally caves and tells us Phoenix's shocking secret.

twenty-eight

Tyler—Jailbird

MY first night in juvenile hall and I'm just trying to keep to myself. I'm not interested in meeting people or telling nosy people my business. In and out that's all I'm about. But I'm quickly learning that old saying that the road to hell is paved with good intentions. After court, I was processed (which took forever) and shoved into a room with three other girls. The moment I walked in the room, these project hoes were looking me up and down like I owed them money or something.

I should've known that when a group of girls are together there are going to be problems. And I just walked into a wasps' nest, because the girl in my top bunk bed is Billie Grant's cousin, Laquisha.

Small world.

For the first couple of hours, Laquisha smiled at me like she thought Christmas had come early. I guess in a way it had for her. Instead of just making her move so we could get some furniture moving around here, Laquisha played her cards close to her chest while she snickered and eyeballed me to death. But soon as the sun started to set and the facility started to thin, I knew trouble was brewing.

Now here I am lying in bed with my eyes wide open, waiting. For what, I'm not sure, but I know that it's coming. Soon.

Another hour passes.

Then another hour.

My eyelids grow heavy. After all, it's been a long day. A lot has happened, and I didn't get that much sleep last night. I fight it as long as I can, but finally lose the war and fall asleep.

A minute later I'm awakened when some bitch wraps a hand around my mouth and hisses in my ear, "We got you, bitch!"

In the next nanosecond, Laquisha starts pounding away on my ribs. I try to swing, only to discover to my horror that they've managed to pin my arms to my sides by tucking the top sheet so tight I'm paralyzed for a full twenty seconds. Ordinarily that's not a long time, but when you're getting your butt kicked it feels like a lifetime. When I finally do get loose, it's on and poppin'. I knock Laquisha's two-hundred-pound ass off me for a few seconds and then get in a few licks with her two skinny friends. For a minute, I'm holding my own—but reality comes back into play, and it's still three against one. Without Kierra and Anjenai as my usual backup, for the first time in my life I actually lose a fight.

It's going to be a long six months.

twenty-nine

Kwan—Falling

Tonight is the night of my big date with Anjenai, and I have to admit I'm actually looking forward to it. I stay up all night spitting rhymes and experimenting with different beats for tonight's open-mike battle at Club Zero. I'm more concerned about impressing Anjenai than I am about winning the contest. The minute I stroll through the school doors, I'm rubbernecking the hallways, hoping to catch a glimpse of Anjenai. She has already given me her number and address so I know where I'm going to pick her up, but I want to catch up with her and make sure that everything is still a go.

While my gaze is wandering, my ear picks up Anjenai's name on the lips of a few girls.

"Giiirrrl! I didn't hardly recognize Anjenai this morning. The hair and makeup—"

"What about her clothes?" the girl's friend says.

"I know. Right? I wonder who she's trying to impress?"

With my curiosity piqued I start to ask the girls where they saw Anjenai when suddenly one of them says, "Oh. There she goes!"

I damn near break my neck trying to turn around. Almost instantly, my gaze crashes into Anjenai and, in turn, my eyes nearly bug out of my head. After that my heart starts pounding hard inside my chest, and after a few more seconds, I have to remind myself to breathe.

From the top, Anjenai's shoulder-length micro braids were gone. Her thick hair is now flat-ironed straight and highlighted with blond streaks. Her face—her beautiful, glowing face—looks as if it is ready for the pages of one of those glossy magazines girls always seem to have their faces shoved into. Eyes poppin', cheeks glowing and her lips—those beautiful strawberry-tinted lips have this brother caught up. In her ears are two silver hoops, around her neck a single silver chain.

Her blouse is this soft lavender number that cuts across her top in a way that for the first time brings attention to a nice cleavage. I ain't going to lie, my gaze sticks there for a minute before it travels on down her slim waist and then to the nice, thick curves that are in a pair of jeans that look as if they were painted on. *Oh, my God!*

I blink a couple of more times to make sure that I'm not dreaming. When it's clear that I'm not, I quickly do a drool check and head straight toward Anjenai with a smile stretched from ear to ear. When she sees me approaching, her lips twitch upward and she starts to slow down. Every eye in the hallway rolls our way, and the idle chitchat grinds to a halt.

A cluster of smooth one-liners swirls inside of my head, but by the time I stop in front of her, they all disappear in a puff of smoke and I'm left standing there in front of her with a deer-in-the-headlights look that's going to do heavy damage to the smooth-swagger act that I've worked so hard to perfect. In the end, Anjenai has to break my hypnotic spell by being the first one to speak.

"Good morning," she says with dimples winking.

"Morning." I rake my gaze over her one more time. "You look…stunning." Instantly, she lights up like a Christmas tree.

"Thanks." Her hand drifts up to her curtain of straight hair. "I figured it was time for a change."

"As long as you like it, then I love it," I tell her—which is true. I like the change, but I was just as smitten by her when she was the cute geek slash athlete. "Sooo are we still on for tonight?" I ask.

"I'm still down," she says. "Are you sure that you still want to pick me up? I don't have a problem with—"

"I'm picking you up," I tell her. "This is a real official date, and we're going to do things the right way."

Anjenai's cheeks darken to a deep burgundy as her smile brightens.

"Are you blushing?"

"A little bit."

Now her entire face has changed color. It's cute and adorable. When I remember that everyone is still watching us, I lean forward and whisper, "So can a brother walk you to your locker?"

"Sure. I don't mind."

Before she starts to walk, I reach over and grab her bag. "Let me carry this for you." Still smiling, she releases the bag and we fall into step side by side, leaving a trail of open mouths in our wake—including Romeo Blackwell's and Phoenix Wilder's.

thirty

Phoenix—Worth Fighting For

HE *still has the hots for that bitch!* I can't believe this. How on earth is this *one* project hood rat able to give me so much grief? What? People are supposed to be impressed because she slapped a hot iron on her hair and put on some makeup? *Puh-lease.* A hood rat is a hood rat is a hood rat. That heifer ain't fooling nobody. I cross my arms and cut my gaze back over to Romeo, waiting for him to put his eyes back into his head and pick his damn mouth off the floor. By the time he does, I have a serious attitude.

"What?" he asks, trying to look all innocent.

"You know what," I hiss. "Don't play me sideways."

"C'mon now. Don't start."

"If you'd stop drooling after that girl, then we wouldn't have a problem, would we?"

He actually has the nerve to roll his eyes. He's lucky I don't try to gouge them out.

"Let's just drop it." He starts toward our homeroom, but I

don't follow him. When he notices this, he huffs out a long breath and rolls his eyes up to the ceiling. "What now?"

"How come you don't ever offer to carry my bags?"

"Are you serious?"

"As a heart attack." I slap a hand onto my hip and work my neck. "Hell, I'm carrying your child, you'd at least think you could handle one measly little bag." Wow. I can't believe I just pushed that lie right out of my mouth with a straight face. Regardless, it gets the desired effect because homeboy waltzes back over to me and takes my bag from me. "Thank you," I say bitingly. "Now, was that so hard?" I roll my eyes and march on to class.

When the homeroom bell rings, we're sitting in the back of the classroom in our usual seats with steam still rising off of my head. Mainly because I can't stop replaying that little scene between Anjenai and Kwan. Not because the bitch has moved on—that part is cool as hell with me—but just because of the reaction of this idiot sitting next to me. How you gonna just disrespect me like that in the hallway? Did he see that once Anjenai and Kwan exited stage left, every eye then rolled to us? Did he seriously think that no one else saw that pathetic little face of his stretching like someone just kicked his puppy? This situation is a real gut check for me. If I tell Romeo the truth about losing the baby, he'll drop-kick my ass to the curb so quick that it will make my head spin. Where would that leave me then?

Sobbing my eyes out in the girls' bathroom.

I slam my eyes shut just thinking about my emotional breakdown a few days back. Just thinking about it now still fills me with shock and amazement. I don't even remember what set that off. I was fine one minute and the next a flood of tears was pouring down my face. Thank God Nicole came when she did. *She…Nicole and Anjenai are friends.* That needling thought keeps poking at me. What if…?

Nah. Nicole wouldn't do that. She promised.

But why would she keep her promise to me? I've been nothing but cruel to her since the day Daddy finally admitted that he even had another child out of wedlock. A child just a year younger than me. Since then I've done nothing but tease her and mistreat her.

Maybe I should go and remind her that blood is thicker than water and I still expect her to keep her word. I mull that over for a minute while Raven and Bianca waltz through the classroom door. I only glance at them for a hot minute and then cut my gaze away. But then I hear a faint whimper and a couple of sniffs and I take another look at my girls. Bianca appears to be upset.

"Anjenai? How could he like that bitch?" she hisses.

Ha! Now the trick knows how *I* feel. Our gazes connect, and before I can roll my eyes in the opposite direction, she shares a look with me that tells how much they miss me. *I knew it. Those bitches are nothing without me.*

Roll call is a brief, uneventful affair, and the moment the last name is marked present, everyone pops out of their chairs and starts visiting friends at other desks including Romeo, who heads over to Shadiq. I need to ease up on him, before we end up fighting and I still lose him.

"Hey, girl," Bianca says to me as she and Raven move to cluster around my desk. "How have you been doing?"

This is a make-or-break moment. I could give these girls

a quick flip of my hair and the back of my head, but the truth of the matter is I miss these bitches' friendship about as much as they've missed mine.

"I've been hanging in there," I tell them, keeping my face neutral.

Raven eases down in the empty chair in front of my desk. "Are you going to Club Zero tonight? Shadiq said that he was performing."

"Shadiq? I thought y'all were swooning over that new kid? What's his name again?"

A pained look ripples across Bianca's face. "Puh-lease. Ain't nobody studin' his weak-rhyming ass," she says un-convincingly. "I'm sure that Shadiq is going to check that ass on the mike tonight."

Raven bobs her head. "Yeah. He's gonna let him know how we do thangs in the dirty-dirty. You know?"

I'm not finished twisting this knife in Bianca's gut just yet. "I don't know. Word around school is that it's going to be a serious battle. Kwan has skills. Plus, he's probably going to be trying to impress some girl he's taking to the joint."

Bianca's pale face drains of what little color she had going. "Anjenai," she spits. "I swear I can't stand that bitch. What the hell do these boys see in that girl?" Her angry glare swings from Raven to me. "Do y'all get this shit, or am I just stuck on stupid?"

"I get it," Raven says, winning our attention. "C'mon. Everybody knows hood girls are easy. The boys wanna roll with these project chicks that be dropping it like it hot and then dropping two, three children before they—*if* they graduate from high school." As soon as she tosses that crap out of her mouths, she slaps a hand over her mouth and swings her gaze back to me.

Bianca tries to quickly repair the damage. "She didn't mean—"

"I'm hardly in the same situation," I inform them, skating the truth. "Romeo and I have been an item for a long time. He didn't meet me one day and screw me the next. We've been planning to be together for a long time. The baby just means that we're going to marry before college and not after. No big deal." I shrug my shoulders. Of course, I need to get him to impregnate me again before I get caught with an empty belly.

"You're so lucky," Bianca says. "I think that it's great that you two have gotten back together."

Raven adds, "Then again, you guys always do."

"Yep. I got my man, so I ain't scared of those nasty project bitches." The girls laugh at my lie while I cut another gaze at Romeo, who still looks miserable. I know without a doubt that he's thinking about Anjenai, and at this moment in time there's nothing that I can do about it.

thirty-one

Kierra—I Will Survive

Anjenai's makeover has turned out to be a huge success. Every hallway I walk down, everyone is talking about her. Of course, if they all knew what the BFFs know, right now they would be talking about Phoenix's trifling and lying ass. Not pregnant? At least, not anymore—and she hasn't been for a minute now. Clearly, she's keeping the lie going because she needs to keep her claws buried in Romeo. That's some foul shit. Especially since most people can take one look at Romeo and know that he's still got it bad for Anjenai.

Anjenai took the news with openmouthed astonishment, but to my surprise she wasn't gung ho about dropping a dime on Phoenix's scheme like I was—hell, neither was Nicole, and I straight up don't understand that. I know if the shoe was on the other foot, Phoenix wouldn't hesitate to stab her in the back. I wish Tyler was here. I know she would side with me on this. Maybe I'll start writing her and letting her know the 411 about all the drama that's floating around here—including my own. McKenya and I still haven't seen hide nor tail of Deborah. Pretty soon, I'm going to have to start doing something that's going to pull money into the house.

From the corner of my eye, I spot Drake huddled up with some dudes, and I wonder if he has a couple more of those caffeine pills. I stroll over to him with a big smile. He looks up just as I'm approaching and tosses me a smile of his own.

"Hey, what's up?" He turns away from some kid, and for a brief moment, I see him stuff a fat knot of bills into his pants pocket. My eyes bulge out on the spot.

"Damn, boy. Is that how you roll?"

He flashes a smile and thrusts out his chest. "Hey, don't let the small size fool you. I'm a first-class businessman. Money moves everything around me just like it does for the rest of the world. You know what I mean?"

I have no idea what he's talking about. "Yeah, man. Cool. Cool."

"So holler at me. What can Brown do for you?"

I laugh at the play off his last name as we turn and start heading toward my locker. "Well, I guess I was wondering if you had any more of those pills you gave me last time. I pulled an all-nighter with some friends, and I know that I'm going to crash and burn before I reach Mr. Griffin's class."

"Ah. I told you those babies would help, didn't I?"

"That they did," I say, grinning at him.

He bobs his head. "I also said that the first package was free. The second one is going to cost you ten."

I blink at him. "Ten dollars for caffeine pills? You tripping." Drake levels a look on me that suddenly brings a lot of stuff into focus. "Those weren't caffeine pills, were they?"

"Not exactly," he says with a halfhearted shrug. "But they were a hell of a pick-me-up, weren't they?"

"You're a drug dealer?"

"Shhh!" He grabs me by the arm and pulls me to the side. "Damn, girl. Why don't you just go ask Ms. Callaway to let you blast it over the intercom?"

I think I'm too stunned to respond. Finally he kicks up another grin at me.

"Looky here. I like you—so this is what I'm going to do." He takes another slick look around and then reaches into his pocket. "I'm going to hook you up with another package."

I shake my head and step away. My mind is reeling. Never in a million years would I have thought that Drake, this quiet, choir-boy-looking kid, was a drug dealer.

"What? Now there's a problem?" he asks, starting to look nervous. "You're not thinking about messing up my hustle, are you?"

I take another step back, but then my eyes fall to the fat knot pressing against the side of his pant leg. *Money.* Drake's eyes follow my gaze. "What? You're thinking about bribing me?"

I shake my head. "No. I'm thinking about you giving me a job."

thirty-two

Nicole—Starving

I ain't even going to lie. This diet is getting harder and harder as the days go by. Last night was a challenge with that big pan of lasagna Kierra baked. My stomach was doing all kinds of growling, but more and more people are noticing the weight loss, so this extreme diet is more than worth it.

Sitting in my first-period American history class, I do start to experience more dizziness. It just came out of nowhere. One minute I'm answering the teacher's question, and the next I feel like I'm riding on the back of a spinning top.

"Ms. Dix. Are you all right?"

I place a hand over my mouth. I think I'm just seconds from hurling those two bites of lasagna I had last night. But thank heavens the bell rings and I'm saved from making an ass of myself. I hightail it out of class so fast, I damn near run Romeo over.

He grabs me by my arm. "Whoa. Whoa. Are you all right?"

"Yeah. I just need to get some air."

Thin concern lines are etched in between Romeo's eyes as he looks me over. "C'mon. I'll walk you outside."

I would've argued with him, but everything is starting to spin again, so I allow him to take me by the hand and lead me outside. Thank God there's a cool breeze going once I step outside. I quickly chug in a few deep breaths and then feel my jittering nerves settle down.

"At least your color is coming back," Romeo says, brushing a few strands of hair out of my face.

Still tugging in deep gulps of air, I flutter a smile at him. "Good to know."

He bobs his head, but there's still concern laced in his eyes. "You look different," he says simply.

"I've been losing some weight," I say. I hope that it didn't come out sounding like I was bragging but I did want him to notice. Instead of praising me, like I secretly hoped he would, his concern deepens. "That wouldn't happen to have something to do with you nearly passing out in class, would it?"

I'm both startled and embarrassed.

"What?"

Cocking his head, Romeo's soft brown eyes meet my own. "You're not doing anything crazy, are you?"

I can't stop the tears from rolling down my face even if I wanted to. Before I know it, he's wrapping his arms around me. "Shh. It's all right."

It's not going to be all right, I want to say. *I'm starving.*

"Look, I know looking a certain way is important and everything with you girls. Hell, with guys, too, now that I think about it. But you know it's not worth harming yourself over. I liked you the way you were."

What? "You did?"

He shrugs. "Yeah. You're much prettier when you're confident in your own skin. So you're a little thicker than the other girls. So what? It doesn't make you a bad person. In fact, I think you're one of the nicest people I know."

All I can manage to do is blink at him.

He smiles and bumps our shoulders together. "I like you."

I blush so hard my face feels like a fireball. "Thanks. I like you, too, even if you are dating my sister." We share a small laugh.

"Good." He links his arm through mine. "What do you say I treat you to some fine dining at one of the snack vending machines in the teachers' lounge?"

"We're not allowed in there."

He gives me another shrug. "Don't worry about it. I have some connections." He winks at me and then leads me back into the building where we immediately bump into the Redbones. Phoenix's gaze zeroes in on me like a laser beam—in particular, Romeo's arm linked through mine. An accusation without words is hanging in the air, and whatever bond I thought that we were forming is severed completely. But I guess she's all right now that she has her girls back by her side.

"Now, where are you two running off to?" she asks, all syrupy sweet.

"Just to go grab something to—"

"You know, Romeo. I need to run to get to class," I say, not wanting to give Phoenix more ammunition.

He swivels his head toward me. "Wait. I want us to finish our talk."

"That's all right." I pull my arm from his. "I really got to get going." He opens his mouth to say something else, but I don't hang around to find out what it is. All I know is that I'm sure to get an earful from Phoenix as soon as she gets my ass alone.

Just great.

thirty-three

Tyler—Defeated

EVERY part of my body is in some kind of pain. Face, chest, arms and legs—you name it, it feels as if I spent the night hurling my body at one Mack truck after another. After Laquisha and her goons finished pounding me into the floor, I spent the remaining hours with the nurse, who made the call that I didn't need to go to the hospital. I beg to differ, because it sure as hell feels as if a couple of things are broken on my body.

Now that it's daylight, this bitch is threatening to send me back to my room, where I assume my attackers are just waiting so we can have another go with what they started last night. To prove that I'm not scared of them I'd have to accommodate whatever bullshit is headed my way, but I'm really looking forward to putting that off as far as possible.

"I swear you girls are just as bad as the boys," Nurse Phillips says, shaking her head and scribbling something in a file.

I don't pay her any attention, but if I had a nickel for every time I've heard that in the past couple of years, I'd be one rich teenager.

"So are you going to tell me what all the fighting was about?" she asks.

"Hell if I know."

Nurse Phillips levels a look on me that says that she doesn't buy it. Why in the hell would I care what she thinks? I just need to map out a plan for how to survive this place for the next six months. Of course I come up with nothing by the time I'm released from the nurse's office and escorted back to my room by some big gorilla-looking woman who probably couldn't smile even if God came down and put in a personal request. When I realize that I'm headed in a different direction, I say, "Isn't my room down the other hallway?"

Gorilla just rolls her eyes. "Since it's clear that you and your roommates don't get along, we decided that it's best that we break y'all up."

Thank God. Maybe now my rib cage can get a little more rest before I have to play Rocky again. But whatever joy I experience in that short trip to my new room is quickly dashed when my *new* roommate looks over to the door and slides on a big greasy smile.

"Well, well, well," she says, sitting up. "I heard your ass was here."

Out of the frying pan and into the fire. "Hello, Billie."

BFF Rule #11

Love, Trust and Support.

thirty-four

Anjenai—Room for Two?

"MY goodness. You're about as nervous as a long-tailed cat in a room full of rocking chairs," Granny declares as she watches me reapply the makeup Kierra taught me how to use last night.

"I *am* nervous," I tell her. "What if you don't like him and the boys set out to embarrass me like they usually do?"

She snickers like that stuff is really out of the realm of possibility. "Chile, that boy is already in good with me. Coming over here and meeting me proper tells me that he at least got some home training—not like that boy you used to sit out in the car with acting like this place was some kind of drive-in movie."

I instantly recall the kiss Romeo gave me in his car out in the parking lot when he drove me home after a night of basketball practice and pizza. Damn, it was just a month ago, but it feels like a lifetime.

"Well, Kwan is different," I tell her. "At least he doesn't have any baby mama drama at fifteen."

"That's more good news." She settles a hand on her hip and cocks her head while I try to line my eyes with one smooth stroke of gel eyeliner.

"What?" I ask, catching an almost goofy grin on her face.

"Nothing." She shakes her head. "I'm just amazed at how fast you're growing up. Dating, next it will be the prom and then you'll be telling me that you're engaged."

"Whoa. Whoa. Let's just get me through the ninth grade," I joke.

"Fine. Fine." She tosses up her hands. "Do you think you have time to take a little of this casserole over to your friend Kierra's before you leave?"

I remove the brush from my eyelid and frown back at her through the refection in the mirror.

"I know we ain't got much to share ourselves, but every little bit helps, I reckon," she says, turning away from the bathroom.

"What are you talking about?" I ask, turning and following her to the kitchen. "Why would Kierra and them need a casserole from us? Is there something going on that I don't know about?"

Granny glances back at me with a surprised look. "You mean you don't know?"

Suddenly, my heart starts pounding in double time. "Know what?"

She just blinks at me as if I'd asked her to explain the birds and the bees to me again.

"Well, honey, if Kierra hasn't told you, then I don't think that it's my place."

Kierra not tell me something? The actual thought of that causes my heart to squeeze so hard that I literally gasp aloud. "Granny, what are you talking about?"

She goes over to the oven and pulls out a casserole dish wrapped in aluminum foil. "Here, baby. Take this on over and ask her yourself. I don't think it's my place to tell you if she hasn't."

"Tell me what?" I feel myself getting agitated.

Instead of answering, Granny hands over the dish, oven mitts and all. "Ask her."

I stare at my grandmother for another full ten seconds, halfway hoping that she will just break down and confess to whatever the heck she's hinting at. No dice. In the end, I take the casserole dish and rush over to Kierra's place. My mind is scrambling in half a million directions trying figure out this great mystery. By the time I knock on the door, my stomach is tied up in knots. Why, after everything we've been through, hasn't she told me about whatever is going on with her? Have I been ignoring her? Have I been so wrapped up in my own world that I haven't been paying attention to her?

Finally, I hear footsteps approach the door. I take a deep breath and tell myself to remain calm and not just start interrogating Kierra when she opens the door.

"Who is it?"

"It's me," I tell her, rolling my eyes and tapping my foot. Why doesn't the girl ever use her peephole on the door?

"Anje?" She slides the chain lock off and then twists the bolt lock before opening the door. "What are you doing here?" she asks. "Aren't you supposed to be on your date? Is something wrong?"

Kierra's instant concern about me quickly wipes away every question I had coming over here. I don't know why, but suddenly small pieces of the puzzle Granny gave me start clicking in place. Pieces I hadn't paid attention to until now. When was the last time I saw Deborah's car parked in the parking lot? There being so little food in the refrigerator last night and her cavalier attitude toward letting me borrow clothes from her sister's closet. Why does it seem as if Kierra is exhausted all the time?

"Anje?" Kierra opens the door a little farther, as if to step outside the apartment, and I catch sight of some guy in the living room with a big duffel bag on the table. I think I've seen him around school, but I'm not sure.

"Oh, I didn't know that you had someone coming," I say. "I can come back another time." I turn and belatedly realize that I still had Granny's casserole in my hand. "Oh. Granny wanted me to bring you this."

Kierra glances down. "What's that?"

"A casserole." I shrug my shoulders up and down. "I guess she, um, made a little too much this evening."

Kierra's brows dip together at my odd answer, but heck, I couldn't think of anything else to say.

"Well, thanks," she says, fluttering a smile. "I'm sure we'll enjoy it since your granny can throw down in the kitchen." She reaches for the dish, but I step back. "Ah, it's hot. I can just take it to the kitchen." Mainly, I want to see if she'll invite me into the apartment or pull another Tyler and leave me standing out here in the hallway.

Kierra does hesitate for a moment, but then finally steps back with that same nervous smile. "Sure, come on in."

Relief pours over me as I take a huge step across the threshold. The dude sitting on the sofa hops up and quickly flips the top of his duffel bag down as if he doesn't want me to see what's inside.

"Oh, hey, Anjenai. How's it hanging?"

Surprised that he knows my name, I take a harder look at his face and try to place a name to it.

"Drake," he answers the unspoken question. "Drake Brown. I go to Jackson High with you and Kierra."

A boyfriend? My smile stretches as I turn an accusatory glance toward my best friend. Her face is bright red with embarrassment.

"C'mon. You can put the casserole on the stove. We'll have some for dinner tonight," she tells me as she turns and marches into the kitchen.

I follow close behind her. "You know you're wrong for this, don't you?" I hiss at her. "Why didn't you tell me you were seeing some dude at school? How long have you two been seeing each other?"

She blinks at me. "Um, we, um, are just friends," she says unconvincingly—mainly because her entire face is blotchy red.

"Uh-huh. You ain't got to front. It's me, remember?" I lean out the kitchen door and take another look at the dude. "He's a little short—but then again, so are you." I wiggle my brows at her. "Where's McKenya?"

"Spending the night at her friend Regina's place. I walked her a few minutes ago."

"Ah. So it's just you and this dude in the house," I say. "You better not let Deborah find out." The words are out of my mouth before I can stop them. In my defense, all I can say is that I wasn't thinking. Also in that one second, Kierra's red face collapses and a rush of tears starts pouring down her face.

"Oh, God, Kierra. I'm sorry." I sweep open my arms and quickly wrap them around her small shoulders. Next thing I know she's drenching my shirt with warm tears. "It's going to be all right," I tell her. "Why didn't you tell me?"

"I didn't want anyone to know," she admits. "What if someone told Child and Family Services and breaks up McKenya and me? What if we have to go to foster care or something?" She starts shaking her head. "I wouldn't be able to stand it. We might not be able to be friends anymore."

"C'mon. That will never happen. We will always be friends no matter what happens."

She continues to shake her head. "We don't know that. I mean, look what's happening between us and Tyler. We're already separating and we've only been in high school a couple of months. I can't imagine what we'll be like after four years."

That thought had also crossed my mind. "Look. We're not going to let that happen," I tell her despite my own doubts. "We're going to do our best not to let that happen. As far as Tyler is concerned, we're going to start writing and sending her care packages every chance we get. Agreed?"

Kierra cries just a little harder.

"If life is going to get harder, then we're just going to fight harder to stay together. Agreed?" I insist.

"Okay," she croaks. "Agreed."

"Good." I walk over to a thinning roll of paper towels. "Now wipe your face. Now, since McKenya is spending the night out, what do you say about going to Club Zero with Kwan and me?"

"What? No...I can't."

"Why not? We can double date." I turn toward the kitchen door.

"Wait...no, Anje—"

"Drake," I call out to the living room, ignoring her. "How do you feel about going out to Club Zero with us tonight?"

"Club Zero?" His face lights up. "Count me in!"

I turn toward Kierra. "There, it's all settled. All we have to do now is tell *my* date."

thirty-five

Kwan—My Girl

I'M so nervous that you would've thought it was my first date. I don't know how many times I changed clothes before I settled on some basic black jeans and a classic white Sean John T-shirt. I want to be fly without looking like I'm trying too hard. I'm comfortable rolling through the hood because what so few people know down here is that I grew up in the Bronx. My family hustled a dollar out of fifteen cents to get where we are today, and none of us will ever forget where we came from.

Cruising into the Oak Hill Apartments and leaning to the side behind my white-on-silver Escalade, I toss a few deuces to a couple of brothers hugged up on the corner and quickly find a parking space outside Anjenai's apartment building. After shutting off the engine, I flip down the visor and check my mug shot to make sure everything is everything before sliding out from behind the wheel and strutting my way up to Anjenai's place. I may be cool on the outside, but trust me, on the inside my heart is racing and I can hardly get my thoughts together. Maybe if I just stick with short sentences, I'll do all right.

Outside Anjenai's door, I cough a few times to clear my throat and stop myself from knocking at least twice because I need a few extra minutes to get myself together.

"Are you Anje's date?" a little voice echoes through the empty hallway.

I look around and finally see two little boys sitting on the staircase with a basketball between them.

"Oh, hello," I greet them, smiling. "I didn't see you there."

The two boys gaze at me. Neither looks too impressed. I instantly like them.

"Where are you taking our sister?" the elder of the two asks.

I clear my throat again. "To this place called Club Zero. You probably never heard of it."

"I've heard of Club Zero," the elder one says, crossing his arms.

"Yeah. Me, too," his mini-me co-signs.

"We may be kids, but we know a few things."

"Ah. Is that right?" I ask, walking over to the staircase and then leaning against the rail. "If that's the case, then maybe you can help me out?"

The younger instantly grows suspicious. "Help you out how?"

"Well, clearly, I like your sister, and I'm sure that she's had plenty of boyfriends—"

"Yeah, right!" the boys spit in unison and then crack themselves up laughing.

"What are you two named?"

The younger opens his mouth only to have his brother slap a hand over it. "That depends on who wants to know."

"Fair enough." I bob my head. "My name is Kwan." I stretch out a hand. "I go to school with your sister."

The elder one looks at my hand and then peers up at me for a long time before he finally slides his small hand into mine. "Hosea," he says. "And this here is Edafe. He's the baby."

Edafe pushes Hosea's hand off his mouth. "I'm not a baby!"

"Are, too." Hosea rolls his eyes.

"Nuh-uh. I'm six years old. I'm a big boy. Even Granny says so!"

Now these two have cracked me up, but before we can continue this conversation, their apartment door jerks open and Anjenai pokes her head out into the hallway. "Hosea and Edafe, Granny wants—OH! Hey!" Her eyes completely light up when they land on me.

"Hey, yourself," I respond, feeling my own face split into a double-decker smile.

She eases out into the hall a little bit. "I hope those two aren't giving you a hard time," she says and then gives them a look that clearly states that they better not be.

"No. No. We were just getting to know one another." I glance down at them. "Ain't that right, boys?"

Two sets of shoulders shrug before popping up from the staircase and then running toward the apartment.

"Well, so much for that," I say, feeling jilted. "I thought we were bonding."

"Please don't take it personally," she says. "They're weird like that."

I bob my head again and then allow a comfortable silence to float between us while I stroll over to the door. I catch a whiff of something flowery clinging to her skin. "You smell nice."

Those adorable dimples wink at me again. "Thanks." We smile at each other for a while before she finally says, "I, uh, hope you don't mind but I kinda, sorta invited Kierra and Drake to come with us."

Stunned, I blink at her.

"I know I should've asked you first, but I just found out that she was going through some really tough, personal things and I wanted her to get out so she can relax some. Please. Please say that you don't mind."

She grabs my hand and gives me such an adorable puppy-dog expression that whatever disappointment I was feeling just melts away. "I don't mind," I tell her, squeezing her hand back. My reward is another breathtaking smile. So far the date is off to a good start.

Anjenai invites me into the apartment and introduces me to her grandmother. I'm really good with grandmothers since I'm really close to my own. I am a little surprised when two more brothers, twins, come out from the back room and are forced to introduce themselves by their smiling grandmother. I keep the discussion light, tell her just the basics about myself before promising to have Anjenai home by eleven o'clock on a school night. Next, we walk over to her girl Kierra's pad and pick her up. I realize I have seen Kierra around school and wonder if she's the same girl Chris has been bragging about. Of course I don't ask in front of her date—a dude I really don't care for. Despite my short time at Jackson High, I know exactly who Drake Brown is and what he does around the school.

"Yo, y'all ready to go?" I ask after all the introductions have been made. Everyone glances at each other, bobbing their heads. We head out the door and all pile into my ride. I was expecting an awkward situation once we're all situated, but that doesn't turn out to be the case. Anjenai and Kierra fall into simple chitchat, and then Drake and I join in.

Turns out that it's a good thing that Drake came along because I get completely turned around, trying to get over to the club on my own. When I checked the place out last time, I rode with Chris. Then the parking lot was, like, half-full. Tonight, the place is jam-packed. "I wonder what's going on tonight," I say as I pull into a parking space.

"Are you kidding me?" Kierra says. "It was all over the school that Shadiq plans to battle you onstage tonight."

Drake bobs his head. "True dat. I got fifty riding on Shadiq myself." He cuts a look toward me. "Sorry, my man. I hardly know you, you understand."

"Sure. Sure. No problem." I roll my eyes. *Just great.* I thought this place was perfect for me to try to get my feet wet—work on perfecting my flow. It's one thing to spit out some rhythms trying to impress Anjenai—it's quite another going head to head with some dude I barely know, thinking that I'm threatening his rep or something.

"Is everything all right?" Anjenai whispers over to me.

"Yeah. Yeah," I lie, shutting off the engine. "I guess it is what it is."

She gives me a look that tells me that she sees straight through my lie, but she's cool enough to let it go in front of her friends. However, when we climb out of the car and head toward the low-key club kitty-corner in an old strip mall, she leans over to my side and whispers, "You know, you don't *have* to do this. We can go somewhere else if you like."

I'd like that very much, but we're here now and I definitely don't want anyone saying that I punked out. The only thing left to do is to grin and bear it. I glance down into Anjenai's upturned face and feel those familiar muscles start to tug at my heart. "It's cool," I say and then swing my arm around her shoulders without thinking about it. It really could be an embarrassing moment, if she chooses to shrug it off. However, to my amazement, she instead tucks herself neatly under my arm and marches in lockstep next to me. I've got a feeling that this is going to be a pretty good date.

No sooner does that thought cross my mind than I look up to open the club door and standing right there in front of us are Romeo and Phoenix. If looks could kill, Anjenai and I would be a couple of chalk outlines right now. The funny part is, this dude is staring a hole in my head while his girl is standing right next to him. Talk about issues.

"Hey, what's up?" I ask just to mess with him. In my arm,

I feel Anjenai tense up a bit, but when I glance down at her, she's smiling up at me—dismissing this fool like yesterday's trash. Romeo just turns straight purple, but I look him dead in his face and dare him to say something. "Excuse us," I say, brushing past him since he seems all tongue-tied and what have you.

Inside the club, the bumping bass immediately gets my heart pounding in the same hypnotic rhythm. Music has always had that effect on me. It's hard to explain, but all I know is that I need it as much as I need air to breathe. We quickly search around the room, looking for a good table, and finally find one sort of in the middle of everything.

"Is this all right?" I ask Anjenai.

She nods, but then she and Kierra go back to looking around the place like two kids at Disney World for the very first time.

"Y'all want something to drink?"

"Drink?" Anjenai asks, surprised. "They let us drink in here?"

I can't help laughing. "Nah. They don't serve *those* kinds of drinks. Non-alcoholic drinks."

"Oh." She looks a little disappointed. "Then I guess I'll get a Sprite."

"One Sprite coming up." I leave the table, but have a hard time making it over to the concessions for all the people stopping me and wishing me well. By the time I make it back, I see our party has expanded by one more person.

"Kwan, do you know my friend Nicole?"

I nod my head even though I don't think we've been properly introduced before. I just know that this little evening for two has now expanded to five. One thing for sure is that no matter where I move I can still feel Romeo's stare burning a hole in the back of my head.

"I hope you don't mind my joining you guys. I just came to hear the battle tonight," Nicole says.

Everybody knew about this battle but me. "Sure. Pop a squat." I sit down next to Anjenai and place her drink down in front of her. "For you, sweetheart."

Those adorable dimples reappear as she thanks me. Despite the crowded club and table, Anjenai and I huddle together and create our own private world so we can talk. She tells me about her life, losing her parents in a bad car accident three years ago and how she and her four brothers had to move in their grandmother's small apartment. I get the Cliff's-Notes history of her and the BFFs. I think it's cool to actually have friends you've known all your life. I don't really have a best friend that I can say that I'm totally down with. Acquaintances, yes. Friends, yes. But not the kind who have been with me through the kind of craziness that it sounds like her and her girlfriends have been through.

Time is just ticking away while we share stories and occasionally bob our heads in time to the music. When the club's DJ takes the stage and announces that it's time for the open-mike portion of the show, everyone jumps out their seats and crowds around the stage. It's time for me to do my thing. I'm both hyped and nervous at the same time. Anjenai picks up on this and leans over and whispers in my ear, "You're going to be great!"

I cock a smile, loving the fact that she has faith in a brother. Feeling comfortable now, I press a quick kiss against her right cheek, watch her blush and then stroll through the crowd to write my name on the DJ's list. Six brothers and one chick take the stage before me and to be truthful, each one of their games is wack. The first four are booed off like amateur night at the Apollo.

The DJ is getting closer to my name, and it occurs to me about the same time I hear some other people whispering that Shadiq is nowhere to be found. Is he not coming? Did he chicken out or just change his mind? I really don't know since I was the last to know we were supposed to be battling in the first place.

The dude before me gets a measure of applause before the DJ jumps back on the stage and takes the mike from him. "All right. All right. Not bad," he says. Straight up I think I've heard this cat in a few ATL rap videos, but I have a hard time placing his moniker, DJ Spock. "We have one more name coming to the stage," the DJ announces, and there's a clear murmur of confusion coursing through the crowd. "I'm told that the brother is new to the ATL area. So straight out of the Bronx, put your hands together and give this cat a big ATL welcome. Everyone, KWAN!"

I hop up onto the stage like Rocky about to go to battle with Apollo Creed. Everyone starts cheering even before I take the mike from the DJ. I have less than a second to find Anjenai's smiling face in the crowd before the beat drops and I lock the rhythm into my head.

Everywhere I go people think they know me
They don't know about my struggle or care about my hustle

They see my shine and think I got it easy
But if they step to me wrong we're going to tussle.

I slow the beat to a 2/4 time.

Keep pushing
Keep hustling
Keep do-ing my thing.

I'm into my zone and I can really tell the crowd is feeling me.

While you're learning the game I wrote
I'm taking you down, brother, note by note
Keep pushing
Keep hustling
Keep do-ing my thing.

I roll my hand along and the crowd joins in on the chorus. I find Anjenai's face in the crowd again, and she's singing and bobbing her head. Our eyes connect and the energy flowing between us is better than any performance high I've ever known. In that moment, I know that she is my girl and I'm her man.

thirty-six

Phoenix—Losing Romeo

NOW, isn't this a hot mess? I watch the look that Kwan and Anjenai share while he's on the stage and settle a hand on my hip. I should be happy that I got that girl out of my hair, but clearly her moving on is affecting my man in ways that are, quite frankly, pissing me off. I'm starting to feel as if I've been cast in some crazy soap opera with so many triangles that we're going to have to start keeping flow charts. I want to keep my man, but he's clearly still in love with Anjenai. Anjenai now wants Kwan, who Bianca likes—and Chris secretly likes Bianca.

Like I said, it's crazy.

I'm tired of Romeo staring Kwan down, so I lean over and yell above the music. "It's getting a little warm, do you mind getting me something to drink?"

Romeo doesn't hear me, so I have to reach over and touch him on the arm to get his attention. When he finally turns toward me, it's as if he's looking straight through me. I swear it's taking everything I've got not to snap, crackle and pop all upside his head. If I do, I'm wrong, but if I let it slide where does that leave me?

"Are you finished gawking at your girlfriend?" Maybe it's the edge in my voice that breaks that glassy look in his eyes because he pushes up from the table and tells me that he'll be right back. Hell, I'm beginning to doubt that the Romeo I've always known and loved will ever come back to me. I watch him move from the table and melt into the crowd.

Kwan has completely taken over the joint by spitting out one rhythm after another. I have to hand it to him: he's good.

Real good.

"I swear I can't stand that bitch!" Bianca thunders, appearing out of nowhere and plopping down at my table. "Are you seeing how she's ogling my man?"

Her man? I nearly burst out laughing at her silly ass with that one.

"Calm down," Raven says, squeezing in between us at the table. "She may have won this round, but no way does she have what it takes to keep a guy like Kwan interested—let alone satisfy him. Ain't that right, Phoenix?"

Their gazes swing toward me, and I have no choice but to smile and nod my head in support, but in my head I'm starting to think we should stop underestimating Anjenai and the power she seems to cast over guys. They seem to drop like flies around her, and I'll be damned if I can figure out why.

After being left hearing Bianca whine and complain for way too long, I cast my gaze across the dancing crowd to see where in the heck Romeo has disappeared off to. I spot him clear on the other side of the room, huddled up again with Nicole. My heart drops.

Why in the hell is she always hanging around him all of a sudden?

You know why.

She wouldn't, I start arguing with myself.

Why wouldn't she?

My one moment of weakness is coming back to bite me on my butt—hard. What on earth was I thinking to trust a secret like mine to a sister I've never really considered a sister in the first place? I continue watching her and Romeo with my stomach twisting into knots at the range of emotions playing across his face.

She's telling him!

No, she can't be.

She's clearly telling him! Look!

Oh, God, please tell me this isn't happening! What the heck do you think he's going to do? My heart starts ramming against my chest. Romeo glances up and meets my gaze.

I smile.

But he doesn't.

Damn it! She told him.

I told you.

Romeo leans over and whispers something into Nicole's ear before he turns away and trudges off. I push away from the table in the middle of Bianca plotting and scheming against Anjenai and her troop of BFFs.

"I'll be right back," I say.

Bianca casts me a hurt look, but I really don't have time

for this. My world is just seconds away from blowing up in my face. I push, shove and walk all over people's feet while trying to make my way over to Nicole. When I reach her, I just grab her by the arm and pull her off the floor.

"Ow. Phoenix. That hurts," Nicole complains as my fingers dig in. I don't pay her any mind. I drag her all the way toward a dark corner away from the crowd.

"How could you?" I stomp my foot at her. "The one time I try to treat you like a sister, you betray me like that?"

"What? I didn't!"

"Don't lie to me! I just saw you tell Romeo! You think I'm blind and stupid?"

"Phoenix, you don't understand."

"Oh, yes I do." I inch closer. "*You've* always been jealous of me. My clothes, money—my friends—"

"Your friends?" she spits. "Trust me. Bianca and Raven are nothing to be bragging about!"

"Oh. And Anjenai and the Section 8 crew are?"

"Yes! Those girls know more about true friendship than you'll ever be able to comprehend. Even when life gets so tough and situations strain and send them in different directions, there's a bond that can never be broken. Becoming their friend has been the best thing that has ever happened to me, and I don't think I have to apologize to you about it. Let's face it, the only reason you confessed your big secret to me is that *your* friends left you high and dry—just like fake friends always do!"

I can't believe it when I feel fresh tears sting and trickle down my face. "You don't know what the hell you're talking about."

"And you're playing with fire, trying to hold on to something—or, rather, someone who doesn't belong to you anymore."

I wave my finger in Nicole's face. "Romeo is not your concern. Stay away from him."

Nicole's eyes narrow as she hisses back, "You don't deserve him. He's too nice a guy to be lied to and manipulated by you. I didn't tell your precious secret—but he's going to find out."

The only thing I hear is that she *hasn't* told Romeo about the baby. My entire body deflates with relief. "I may have lost Romeo's baby a few weeks ago, but you can best believe I'll have him knock me up again before long. Boys are easy that way. You, on the other hand, if I so much as see you breathe in his direction again, I'll make your life pure hell. You feel me?"

Nicole calmly folds her arms with a self-assured smirk that I want to just smack off her face.

"Don't believe me? Try me!"

I whip around to storm away but freeze dead in my tracks when I see Romeo standing just a couple of inches away and glaring at me with a murderous look. "What the hell do you mean that you lost the baby a few weeks ago?"

thirty-seven

Romeo—Unchained.

Please *tell me that I didn't hear her right.* But Phoenix's declaration loops inside my brain a few hundred times in quick succession until I'm dizzy.

"A few weeks ago?" I step back, overwhelmed with so many emotions it's damn near impossible to name them all. But anger and betrayal are stinging me the most.

"Romeo, I can explain," Phoenix says, moving toward me. For every step she makes, I take two back. I have to—or I'm going to hurt this girl.

"Romeo!"

"NO!" I suddenly remember the buffalo wings I bought for Nicole because she looked like she was just seconds from passing out on the dance floor and I had guessed that she's been starving herself to lose the amount of weight she has in such a short period of time. I almost toss them into the garbage because if I understand the argument between the sisters, Nicole knew about Phoenix losing the baby and she didn't say a word to me. I've always thought of her as a friend.

But when my gaze cuts over to Nicole, I see regret and remorse written across her face. It's hard being mad at Nicole. She always tries so hard to fit in. I move around Phoenix and hand Nicole her food.

"Here. Promise you'll eat this."

She blinks and takes the food. "I—I promise."

I nod and start to storm off.

Phoenix drops a hand on my shoulder and I jump away from her as if it was a hot poker. "DON'T," I warn her. "As far as I'm concerned we have nothing else to say to each other."

Phoenix's eyes fill with tears, but she's crazy if she thinks it's going to change anything between us. "You have pulled some pretty bat-shit crazy stunts in the past, but this is an all-time low even for you. I'm not even sure that I want to know *how* you lost the baby. Because…because I will never be able to trust anything you say. *Ever. We're through! Finished! Done!*"

"Romeo"

"SAVE IT!"

"Please, Romeo," she sobs. "Don't leave. I can't lose you!" She tries to touch me again, but I flinch away.

"I mean it, Phoenix! Stay the hell away from me. It's over!" I turn and storm away, not caring about the small crowd that has gathered around us. I feel nothing but pure hatred toward Phoenix, and I don't see that ever changing.

I storm through the crowd, not really seeing how everyone just instantly parts away after one look at my face. But there's one thing—or, rather, one couple that catches and holds my attention on the dance floor: Anjenai and Kwan. They're lost in their own world while rocking to a slow song. From a distance they look like newlyweds, smiling and gazing into each other's eyes.

Like several times before, jealousy starts to eat at me like a cancer. If I hadn't gotten caught up in Phoenix's web of deceit I would be the one Anjenai was looking up to at this moment. She would be in my arms. My girl.

I watch them dance until the end of the song, pathetically longing for Anjenai to glance over and see me—want me. But when that doesn't happen I console myself with the knowledge that I'm not just going to let Kwan have her.

No way.

No how.

★ ★ ★ ★ ★

Stay tuned for Book 3 of the BFFs series.

QUESTIONS FOR DISCUSSION

1. The BFFs keep finding that it's harder to keep their original bond intact now that they're in high school. Have you ever been in a situation where you question whether you've outgrown a relationship?

2. Phoenix takes drastic steps to hold on to an old boyfriend. Do you know someone who feels they have to manipulate people in order to get what they want? How do you handle such people?

3. Anjenai has picked herself up, dusted herself off and moved on to the new boy in school. Do you think it's healthy to move from one relationship to another one so quickly? Is Kwan the real deal or just the rebound?

4. Tough girl Tyler has landed in a place where she's not the only girl with a major chip on her shoulder. Is it possible that her time in juvenile hall will finally turn her around?

5. Nicole has been losing weight on a starvation diet. Have you or do you know of anyone who felt they had to use such drastic measures? What were the end results? What do you think they'll be for Nicole?

6. Kierra's older sister seems to be MIA. Is she right or wrong for trying to hide this information from the au-

thorities? Should she have at least told her best friends what's happened? Do you think Deborah will return?

7. It looks like Romeo and Kwan are going to be fighting over the same girl. Who do you think will win and why?

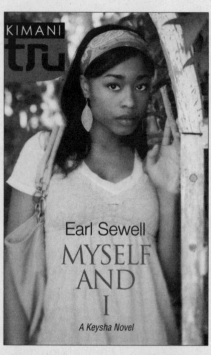